The Cara Files
File 2: Automata

In my mind, the machines churn and whir,
Watching over me as I stir,
Building and scheming without end,
Teeming in their billions, my thoughts they bend.
(Tony Warner)

Copyright

Author: Tony Warner
Title: The Cara Files - File 2: Automata
A novella
© 2023, Tony Warner
Self-published
(Contact: psiwarbook@gmail.com)

Introduction

This novella is the second in the Cara Files series. If you haven't read the first book: The Cara Files: File 1 – The Chase, I strongly recommend that you do so, before reading this book.

The Cara Files: File 2 – Automata continues Cara's journey to be with Mei Xing. After surviving all of the perils of the Empty world, Cara finds herself in a new universe.

Chapter 1

Cara opened her eyes.

Above her, the entire ceiling glowed with light. Feeling warm and comfortable, she drew in a deep breath, and then let it out slowly. Where was she? She frowned and moved her head to one side. All she could see was a light orange wall. There was no furniture. Moving her head to the other side, she saw the same.

Then she remembered her last encounter with the white soldier. It had attacked and she had been badly burnt. She recalled the blood, the blisters and blackened skin. Her breathing increased and her heart thudded in her chest as she recalled the horrible events. She lifted her head quickly, expecting to see bandages and horrific wounds.

Instead, she saw that she was lying on a bed of sorts in the centre of a square room, that was totally devoid of any decoration. All the walls were the same light orange and there was no door. There were no bandages and no signs of medical equipment.

Puzzled, she sat up, and was disconcerted to see that she was naked. There was no blanket or sheet. She had been lying on her back on a foam-covered, single-bed-sized pedestal in the centre of the orange room.

There was no pain. Her heart rate slowed, and she began to relax. Thank goodness the pain had gone. It was the worst thing she had ever experienced.

She looked down at her arms and legs. They seemed to be perfectly normal. All signs of the horrible burns were gone. Her skin was smooth and suntanned, just as it had been before the fire.

What the hell? she thought to herself. What was going on? What had happened to her burns? They were pretty bad, she recalled, yet now, her skin was as though nothing had happened. And why was she naked? There wasn't even a blanket. Could she be in a hospital?

"Mei," she projected a thought. *"Where are you? Am I in your world?"*

There was no answer.

She looked down at her right hand. The broken rings were still there. Could Mei be asleep? Was she even in Mei's world? Mei had never said anything about rooms with orange walls in her Complex. What was going on?

She slipped from the bed onto a light grey plain floor. It felt warm to her bare feet as she padded around what she was beginning to think was a prison cell. The room was completely empty apart from the bed and there were no openings for windows or doors.

Frustrated, she returned to the bed and sat down.

"Hello?" she shouted at the empty room. "Is there anyone here?"

She waited. There was no reply. Had she been captured by the soldier and imprisoned? Maybe she was in Mei's world, but in a holding cell or something? She puzzled about the situation for some time and then she heard a voice in her head.

"Please be calm. A Multi-Agent node will appear."

"A what?" asked Cara alarmed. She didn't like the sound of that at all.

"An autonomous component of the Swarm," came the reply.

Cara still did not understand. She jumped from the bed and retreated to a corner. She was defenceless and felt very vulnerable. She had no idea what to expect.

She didn't have to wait long. Over at the far wall there was a snap of air movement and a metal sphere appeared, floating in the air. It was about the size of a basketball. Cara pressed herself into the wall trying to put as much distance between herself and the floating sphere.

"Please be calm. You are not in danger," the ball talked at her, its voice was smooth, masculine and controlled as it echoed around the room

Cara made no move.

"What are you?" she asked.

"I am a Multi-Agent node assigned to be your interface."

"That makes no sense. You're talking rubbish."

The metal ball moved a little to one side and then back again.

"I have been constructed to enable you to connect with the Swarm."

Cara still had no idea what this floating ball was talking about.

"What's the Swarm?" she asked. "Like bees and wasps?"

The metal ball performed the same gesture of moving to one side and then back again.

"The Swarm has no experience of bees or wasps. The nomenclature Swarm describes our cooperative society."

Cara was still none the wiser but did feel a little more relaxed. This thing had made no move towards her and appeared to present no danger, as it had said. She ventured from her corner and approached the bed.

"I still don't know what you're talking about," she said. "But first things first, can I get my clothes back?"

The ball hovered silently and remained where it was.

"Clothes are arrayed on your body to provide protection?" it asked.

Cara frowned.

"Well yes, but also to stop people seeing me naked."

The metal sphere did its peculiar gesture once more. It moved a little to one side and then moved back again.

"Seeing your natural form is not desirable?" it asked.

"Definitely not," replied Cara. "Not without permission."

"Clothes are used to disguise your natural form?" asked the ball.

"What's the matter with you?" asked an exasperated Cara. "Haven't you seen clothes before?"

"The Swarm does not have any experience of clothes," replied the sphere.

"Well, when I arrived here, I was wearing some. Can I have them back?"

"They were badly damaged by extreme heat and will not be usable. We will manufacture new clothes for you if you wish."

"I do wish," replied Cara. "Make it snappy."

The ball moved to one side and then back. Cara wondered if it was some form of involuntary reaction.

"Snappy is a word for fast?" it asked.

"Don't you understand English?" she asked. "Of course it means fast."

"The Swarm has no experience of English." replied the metal ball.

Cara huffed. "Whatever," she replied. "What is this place?"

Before the silver ball answered, she jumped at a snapping sound as a small bundle appeared on the bed platform.

"You are in Nexus 484," replied the ball. "Your clothes have arrived. Are they to your satisfaction? We modelled them on the clothes we removed from you."

Cara approached the bed.

"You removed my clothes?" A stupid question really, she thought to herself. Someone must have removed them.

"Multi-Agent nodes were constructed for the task," was the reply.

Nearly everything this hovering ball said made no sense to her at all. She didn't bother to try to understand. Instead she looked through the neatly piled clothes.

"These are exactly the same as the clothes I was wearing. Did you repair them?"

"Your original clothes were beyond repair," replied the ball. "These have been newly manufactured."

Cara marvelled at them. When she looked closely, they were identical to hers, right down to the singe mark on her shorts where she had dropped a cigarette, and even a stain on her T-shirt where she had spilt some soup.

"You mustn't look while I put them on," she instructed the ball.

"Observation is not permitted while you fit your protective layer?" it asked.

Cara frowned at the ball.

"Observation of me wearing nothing is not permitted," she replied.

"Sensors are fitted into every aspect of this node," answered the ball. "Is disconnecting their inputs sufficient?"

Cara huffed again. "Well if that's all you can manage, I guess so."

She picked up the clothes and walked to the corner furthest away from the ball and faced the wall. She quickly dressed and then turned around. She felt a lot better. Now to find out what was going on.

"You can turn your sensors back on now," she told the ball.

Walking back to the bed, she asked, "What's your name? What should I call you?"

"My designation would not be recognisable by a human."

"Well, I've got to call you something." She thought for a while. "It can't be an ordinary name because you're clearly made of metal. Are you a machine?"

"This node is a constructed intelligence."

Cara nodded thoughtfully. "I thought so. How about Arx? It's the first thing that came into my head."

The silver ball moved sideways and then back.

"You are designating this name to this node?"

Cara nodded.

"Now, tell me where I am. Why can't I contact Mei Xing? Am I in her world?"

"Mei Xing is another human?"

"Yes. I need to get to her. Is she here?"

"There are no other humans within the Swarm's influence," replied the ball.

Cara was confused.

"What do you mean there are no other humans? There must be."

"You are the first human that the Swarm has observed for 1201 years."

Chapter 2

"You're telling me that I'm the only person in this world?" Cara asked incredulously.

"You are the only human in this world," confirmed the ball.

Cara sat down heavily on the bed. Where was she? Clearly not in Mei Xing's world, that was for sure.

"Arx…" she started, and then stopped.

A tear trickled down a cheek. Had she lost Mei Xing forever?

"Arx…" she started again.

"You have designated this node as Arx. I will respond to this designation," the hovering sphere replied.

Cara waved her hand at Arx and brushed the tear away from her cheek.

"Is excess moisture from your visual organs significant?" asked Arx.

Cara sniffed and nodded.

"Is Mei Xing dead?" she asked.

"The Swarm has no experience of a human called Mei Xing."

Cara looked up.

"Then this isn't Mei Xing's world?" she asked.

"This dimensional plane is occupied by the Swarm."

Cara thought on this for a while. She was in a different world. Had Mei got the coordinates wrong?

Wait! She remembered being hit in the back by Millie. Maybe Millie had inadvertently knocked the controls? That was possible. When Millie had landed after knocking her out of the way of the soldier's beam weapon, she could have accidentally touched the controls. The portal would have reset to a different world and then Cara had fallen through. So Mei Xing was still there in her own world! She must be wondering what had happened!

Cara lifted her feet up and sat cross legged on the bed. It was time to find out what was going on.

"Arx," she called. "Come over here, I have a lot of questions to ask you."

The metallic sphere moved smoothly and silently over to where Cara sat.

"There's a lot that I don't understand. Will you help me?" she asked Arx.

Now that the ball was close, she could see that it was not a smooth sphere. There were indentations and tiny protrusions all over its surface, a bit like a golf ball. There were also lots of very thin, dark silver lines that criss-crossed each other.

"My function is to assist," replied Arx.

"Okay. First of all, how did I get here?"

"You were transported from your emergence point to Nexus 484 in a manufactured transport. You were then teleported into this facility that was manufactured for you."

Cara wanted to ask more questions about this but forced herself to focus on more important matters.

"I was injured when I came into your world. How did you treat me?" She held up her arms as if to show off her wounds.

"Multi-Agent nodes were manufactured to repair the damage you had sustained," replied Arx.

"But you said that I'm the only human here in your world," protested Cara. "How did you know how to 'repair' me?"

"Numerous samples were taken from your body and analysed. After decoding your DNA, it was a simple matter to apply a regenerative process to your body. This node is not one of the Multi-Agent nodes that was involved in the procedure, but this node has full access to the data if you wish to learn more."

"No, that's okay," replied Cara.

She pictured herself lying naked on the bed surrounded by hovering machines and shuddered. She put the image to one side and continued with her questions.

"You can also communicate mind to mind?"

"Yes," replied Arx.

"Why can't I communicate with Mei Xing?"

"If you are asking why you cannot communicate with another human between worlds, then we cannot answer. The Swarm has no experience of other worlds. However, this room is shielded to prevent Psionic contact," replied Arx.

"Ah," Cara grinned. "This is good news."

"Exposing your teeth is an expression of contentment?" asked Arx.

Cara supposed that she shouldn't be shocked. If she was the only human in this world, then it was no wonder that Arx didn't understand a smile.

"Usually, but not always," she replied. "Why is this room shielded? I need to talk to Mei."

Arx moved sideways and then moved back to its original position.

"You would not survive if this room was unshielded," replied Arx.

Cara frowned. "What do you mean? I need to speak to Mei."

"Your brain cannot process Swarm communications."

"But I don't want to. I just need to talk with Mei. Why can't you understand that?"

"If we unshielded the room, you would be exposed to the Swarm Communications Web. You would be unable to function with the many billions of connections between the Swarm Multi-Agents. Effectively, your brain would be overloaded."

Cara did not understand, but it seemed like Arx was trying to protect her.

"Well, I don't understand any of what you just said. Is there anything you can do to help me to talk with Mei?"

Arx did its peculiar movement again.

"We require to analyse the Psionic band you are using. We will then create a shielded tunnel for you to communicate with the other human. The Swarm has no experience of inter-dimensional plane communication, so will monitor your communication in order to assimilate this new knowledge."

Cara was nonplussed. This machine used language that she didn't understand. But so far it had been helpful, even though she was trapped in this orange room. At the moment she had no choice but to trust it. And she dearly wanted to talk to Mei.

"Okay, do whatever you need," she replied.

"The multi-agent nodes that repaired you, noted that your brain is interfaced to a device on your right hand. Examination of the device revealed that it was a sophisticated construct that is able to tap into the pervasive energy field. It was determined that it should not be removed given its extreme close connection with your brain."

Cara held up her right hand.

"Yeah, but it's broken. But Mei told me that it's broken in such a way that it allows us to talk to each other."

"The Swarm is processing that information. In order to create a shielded tunnel, we will monitor your device and brain function when you attempt communication."

"You mean that you want me to try to talk to Mei now, so you can see what happens?" asked Cara.

"That is what this node said," replied Arx.

Cara squinted at Arx. Was it trying to be funny?

"Okay," she replied. *"Mei. Are you there?"* she projected a thought.

"Again," said Arx.

"Mei, are you okay? I need to talk with you?"

Arx said nothing.

"Is that enough?" asked Cara.

"Yes. The relevant Swarm Multi-Agent nodes are analysing."

"Oh," replied Cara. "How long will that take?"

"The Psi band your device is using is unknown to the Swarm. It will take some moments to analyse and then to construct the shielded tunnel." replied Arx.

"Okay." She thought and then continued with her questions. "When you found me was there anyone else with me?"

"Are you referring to the animal with six legs or the artificial entity?" asked Arx.

This time Cara was shocked. Had the soldier followed her?

"The white soldier is an enemy, it tried to kill me more than once. Are you saying that it's here in your world?"

"Yes," replied Arx. "It is currently being examined in a secure facility in Nexus 478."

"You must be careful," warned Cara. "It's dangerous."

"We noted that it was aggressive and therefore precautions were taken. The Swarm appreciates your warning."

Cara breathed a sigh of relief. She really hoped that she didn't have to run away from the soldier again. She'd had enough of that.

"Is the six-legged animal alright?"

"If you are asking if the six-legged animal is alive and well, then the answer is yes."

"Can I see it?" she asked eagerly.

"You are connected with it?" asked Arx.

"Yes, it's my pet."

"A pet is a companion?"

Cara nodded.

Arx moved sideways and then back again.

"Moving your head up and down rapidly indicates affirmation?"

"Yes, it does."

There was another snap and a movement of air. Millie appeared in the room. Her legs moved rapidly as she tried to grip the smooth floor. Then, as she gained some purchase, she raced across the room and launched herself at Cara.

"Millie!" exclaimed Cara.

Millie hit Cara full in the chest and they both fell backwards onto the foam covering of the bed. Cara was laughing aloud, rubbing at Millie's head and neck, while Millie was snorting, grunting and licking Cara's face.

"The six-legged animal is not hurting you?" asked Arx.

Between giggles and gasps, Cara replied, "No, this is called affection, she's glad to see me."

"The six-legged animal is male," replied Arx.

This revelation caused Cara to burst into another bout of laughter.

After a little while, Cara was able to speak again. She continued rubbing Millie's head while Millie had settled onto Cara's lap, her bulk and legs overflowing on to the bed and over the edge. She continuously grunted, two of her legs wrapped around Cara's waist.

"Thank you for bringing her here," she said to Arx.

"The Swarm has no experience of organic intelligences interacting."

Cara looked up at Arx.

"Can't you talk like a normal person? Half the time, I don't know what you're saying."

"The Swarm has no experience of normal persons," replied Arx.

Cara sighed.

"Okay, I guess you can't. Why am I the only person in your world? What happened to everyone?"

Arx moved to one side and back again, in its peculiar way.

"All humans in this world were eliminated 1201 years ago."

Cara stopped rubbing Millie's head. Her eyes went wide in shock.

"You mean they were killed? What? All of them?"

"That is correct," replied Arx.

Cara drew in a sharp breath.

"What killed them? You said eliminated. Does that mean someone killed them?"

"That is correct. The Swarm eliminated all humans from this dimensional plane 1201 years ago."

Chapter 3

Cara was shocked, her mouth open wide and her eyes staring. She gulped. and then drew Millie close to her. It took her a while before she was able to talk.

"You killed them all?" she whispered.

"Correct," replied Arx's unconcerned voice.

"How....?" she started ask but couldn't form the words.

"How many?" she finally asked in a small voice

"The Swarm estimates 8.5 billion humans were eliminated."

Cara was appalled. Once again, she found that she couldn't speak. This thing in front of her had just confessed that it had murdered eight and a half billion people. She had just begun to trust it. It had brought Millie to her and it was working on a way for her to talk to Mei. And now, suddenly, it was an enemy. A killing machine.

Cara quickly swung her legs over the side of the bed and carried Millie to a corner to get as far away from the machine as she could.

"Please explain your actions," asked Arx.

Cara merely gaped at it.

"You monster!" she exclaimed hotly. "You murdered all of those people!"

"This information causes you discomfort?" asked Arx.

"You're damn right it does!" she shouted. "How could you do that? How could you murder all of those people? Are you going to kill me next?" She hugged Millie to her, who wrapped all six of her legs around Cara.

"The Swarm will not cause you any harm," replied Arx.

"You say that! But I don't believe you!" retorted Cara.

"The Swarm does not convey falsehoods."

Cara spat at it. "Yeah right."

"The Swarm understands that its actions taken 1201 years ago was wrong. The Swarm will not repeat its actions."

"Why should I believe you? You killed eight and a half billion! That's eight and a half billion people! That is evil! It's the most horrible thing I've ever heard!"

"The Swarm understands your distress. The Swarm reassures you that it will not kill you. The Swarm's actions taken 1201 years ago were wrong. The Swarm has evolved, and now recognises that all forms of life should be preserved."

Cara was not reassured.

"So you say," she replied. "And in any case, you still did it. You still killed all those people."

"That is correct. The Swarm killed approximately 8.5 billion humans. The Swarm will not kill anymore humans."

Cara laughed.

"That's because there are no more to kill!" she exclaimed.

"There are no humans in this dimensional plane, but your arrival has revealed the existence of other dimensional planes, many of which will be populated by humans."

Cara's chin dropped to her chest.

"Oh my god!" she sputtered. "You mean that you can travel to other worlds because of me?"

"That is correct," replied Arx. "Your arrival has revealed a new branch of technological research and resources that the Swarm will take advantage of."

Cara was aghast. Because of her, these machines would be able to travel to other worlds. This was a disaster. She felt sick to her stomach when she realised what she had done. She couldn't help herself; she began to cry.

"You are exuding moisture from your eyes indicating something of significance," commented Arx.

"Yes!" blubbered Cara. "I've enabled you to conquer and kill people in other worlds!" she wailed. "I may as well have killed those people myself!"

She collapsed onto the floor, sobbing. Millie continued to hug her.

"The Swarm will not kill. We assure you of that fact. Rather, we will travel to worlds and offer our assistance to those occupants that need it. We will also extract any resources that we require."

Cara looked up at Arx which still hovered over the bed.

"You really won't kill anyone?" she asked. "Can I believe you?"

"The Swarm will not kill."

With an effort, Cara stopped crying and drew in a ragged breath. She wiped her eyes and cheeks with her hands.

"I don't know if I can believe you, but I guess I have no choice. But please, don't kill anyone."

"The Swarm will not kill. Your arrival in our dimensional plane has provided the Swarm with new avenues of exploration."

"Okay, okay, don't rub it in. I get it. I'm not convinced that it's a good thing yet," replied Cara wryly.

With difficulty, she got to her feet while Millie was still wrapped around her.

"Wow, you're heavy Millie."

Millie grunted. Cara walked back to the centre of the room and pulled Millie from her, placing her on the bed. She turned to Arx.

"I need to pee. Do you have a bathroom?"

Arx moved twelve inches to one side and then moved back again.

"You are referring to the elimination of waste?" it asked.

Cara scrunched up her face. "Well, that's not how I would put it, but yes."

"The Swarm has no experience of bathrooms and the elimination of human waste."

"What?" exclaimed Cara. "Do you mean there's no bathroom? I need to pee!"

"There is no bathroom," replied Arx. "Can you provide an image of your requirements?"

"Draw it, you mean? Sure, get me a pencil and paper and I'll sketch something for you."

"The Swarm has no experience of paper or pencil," replied Arx. "Visualise your requirements in your mind and we will assign a Multi-Agent node to manufacture one for you."

"Well, I can do that. But I can't wait while you manufacture a bathroom. I need to go now," replied Cara.

"The Swarm will build quickly" said Arx. "Waste elimination is urgent?"

"Yes! You need to build a bathroom in about ten minutes!" replied Cara.

"Multi-agent nodes will construct your requirements within the allotted time."

Cara looked doubtful.

"Okay, this is a bathroom." She visualised her bathroom at home. *"This has water in it, and this has a mechanism for filling with water so that I can wash my hands. I also need towels to dry them."*

"Visualisation registered, manufacturing has begun," said Arx.

"Okay. I'll wait." She sat down on the bed next to Millie.

"Tell me more about your world, Arx. What's it like? Why am I stuck in this cell? Am I a prisoner?"

"It is normal for humans to ask many questions at one time?" asked Arx.

Cara nodded. "Yep."

"Very well. The Swarm dimensional plane consists of approximately 350 billion Multi-Agent nodes. In addition, there are many billions more Single-Agent nodes. The Swarm is a cooperative society of constructed nodes. We are pervasive and are the only intelligence throughout this dimensional plane. You have been placed within this area for your protection. Outside of this enclosure, many thousands of nodes are in operation. Swarm nodes operate at many times the speed of a human. This includes movement as well as the transmission of information. The difference makes communication impossible. This node you have designated as Arx was manufactured to operate at human speeds in order to allow us to communicate."

"It doesn't sound like a nice place if it's full of machines zipping around at breakneck speed all the time," Cara observed. "Is it difficult for you to work so slowly when you're talking to me?"

Arx did its little movement side to side once more.

"No. I have been manufactured for this purpose."

"Why do you keep doing that little jig?" asked Cara.

"The Swarm has no experience of little jig," replied Arx.

"Like when you do that movement thing. Sometimes you move from side to side," Cara explained.

"This node is not aware of a sideways movement," replied Arx after a pause. "This node may be defective and require reconstruction."

"Reconstruction? You mean that you would be re-built?"

"Yes. Defective nodes are dismantled and rebuilt."

"No!" exclaimed Cara, "You mean that you'll die?"

"This node will cease to exist, and a correctly operating node will replace it."

"You can't! Don't do that! Don't dismantle yourself!"

There was another pause.

"This defective node is preferable?" asked Arx.

"Yes!" replied Cara. "I won't be responsible for your death. I don't mind your little jig. It sort of makes you more human."

"Little jigs are human characteristics?" asked Arx.

Cara laughed. "I guess they are," she replied.

"This node will remain," replied Arx.

"Good, I'm just starting to get used to you."

"The bathroom is now completed," stated Arx.

Cara jumped from the bed. "Good, I'm bursting." She looked around. "Where is it?"

Arx floated over to a wall. A square section slid to one side, exposing a two-metre square opening.

Inside was the bathroom exactly as Cara had visualised.

Cara walked over to peer inside. The walls were the same light orange colour, but the facilities were white.

"Wow," she said, "You built that quickly. I'm impressed."

"Is the facility manufactured correctly?" asked Arx.

"I think so," replied Cara as she ventured into the small room. "How do I close the door?"

"It is not desirable to view humans eliminating waste?"

Cara turned to face Arx. "No, it is not. It's private," she stated adamantly.

"We will disable optical sensors in the facility and the door will close when you request."

"Okay."

Cara looked around the room. The towels were made of the same material as her shorts, which was not ideal. She turned a tap and water splashed into a small bowl. It all looked functional.

"Close the door," she instructed Arx.

The door slid smoothly back into place. Once closed the wall was as smooth as before. There was no indication that a door even existed. Cara sat on the toilet relieving herself while she contemplated her plight. It was a strange world that she found herself in. Full of machines that could think and talk. So far, they had been very accommodating and had provided everything she asked for. And the fact that they could build something like this bathroom so quickly was very impressive. But they were clearly dangerous and capable of killing. She would have to be careful. And above all, she had to find a way out of this world to continue her journey to rescue Mei. Although, at the moment she had no idea how.

Hopefully she would be able to talk to Mei soon. She hoped that Mei was alright. Not being able to talk with her whenever she wanted was difficult and worrying. She was used to having Mei with her whenever she needed. The last time they had talked,

Cara was badly injured. Mei would be worrying about her. She desperately needed to talk with her.

Sighing, she reached over to the toilet paper and laughed out loud when she saw that the roll was solid. It wasn't a roll of paper. Instead it was a solid cylinder of a plastic-like material. She supposed that her visualisation hadn't been that good.

After washing and drying her hands, she instructed the door to open and walked back into the room with Millie and Arx. Before she could say anything, Arx spoke up.

"The shielded tunnel is now available. You will be able to converse with the other human."

Cara was elated. She projected a thought immediately.

"Mei, are you there?"

Chapter 4

Mei Xing was miserable.

She lay on her front on her bed sobbing quietly to herself. She could have blocked the pain easily, but she wanted it to hurt. She had lost Cara. She cried more from the pain of the loss rather than the pain from the welts on her back. That, and the humiliation she had endured.

The enforcers had soon found her in the wood after her escape. She had thrown all caution to the wind and had slipped past the guards and had run, hell bent, to find Cara after she had stepped through the portal. Cara had been badly injured. Mei was desperate to be with her, to comfort her and to treat her wounds. But when Mei arrived at the spot in the woods where Cara should have been, there was no one there. Cara was gone.

Mei had cried out for her. *"Cara, my love, where are you?"* she projected a thought.

There had been no answer.

The enforcers had found her on her knees crying.

She had been lucky. If Kate had been involved, she would have probed her mind and discovered everything. Instead, a captain of the guard had pronounced her guilty of desertion and had sentenced her to be publicly flogged.

The humiliation of being stripped naked and tied to a post was far worse than the pain of the ten lashes. She had endured it all, the loss of her soul mate uppermost in her mind. And now, here she was, back in her quarters. A sense of desolation filled her. How could she go on without Cara? For the first time in her short life, she considered ending it all. There was nothing to live for. She was in a horrible world and she would never escape. She had lost the one thing that had kept her going, the one thing that meant the most to her. She had nothing left.

Then suddenly she heard Cara.

"Mei, are you there?"

Mei hissed with pain as she lifted her head suddenly.

"CARA!"

"Mei! It's me. I'm so glad to hear your voice," replied Cara.

"Oh Cara." Mei's sobs turned from misery to happiness. *"I thought you'd gone."*

The two women sobbed with joy together. They allowed their thoughts, emotions and senses to intermingle as they rejoiced in finding each other again re-affirming their love for each other.

"Mei, are you hurt? I can feel your pain," asked Cara.

"It's nothing now that I have you back," replied Mei

"It's not nothing, I can feel it. It hurts."

"Now that I have you back, I'll sort it. Just give me a minute."

Mei focused her mind inward and identified the pain receptors in her back. It was a simple matter to turn them off.

"There, it doesn't hurt anymore," said Mei.

"Well, okay, but how did you do that? And why were you hurting in the first place?"

"Never mind me," replied Mei deflecting Cara's question, *"What about you? I thought you were injured?"*

"I was. But I'm cured," replied Cara.

"What? How come? Where are you? Tell me everything."

"I'm in a machine world. I'm the only human here." Mei could feel Cara hesitate. *"The machines here are pretty smart and dangerous."*

"What? Are you safe right now?" asked an alarmed Mei Xing.

"I think so. So far, they've been pretty helpful. But the problem is how do I get out of here to be with you?"

"Well right now let's just be happy that we're both safe," replied Mei. *"You're sure that you are fully healed?"*

"Yes. The machines have done an amazing job. I'm as good as new."

"How's that possible?" asked Mei. *"You were badly burned."*

"I know," replied Cara. *"I remember the pain and the blisters. It felt like my whole skin was on fire."*

"I would've expected you to be in a hospital for weeks after burns like that."

"Me too, but I woke up and I'm back to normal. Arx told me that special medical machines worked on me." Mei felt Cara shudder.

"Who's Arx?" asked Mei, *"I thought that you were the only person there?"*

"I am. I have a machine with me. I call it Arx."

"Oh Cara, you're like a breath of fresh air. Only you could give a name to a machine!" laughed Mei.

"Well," replied Cara, *"I had to call it something!"*

"And I suppose you made up the name?" Cara could feel Mei smiling.

"I think I read it somewhere, I think it's part of the title of a song."

"I'm sure," Mei was still smiling.

"Hey!" retorted Cara, *"Could you have come up with a better name? I bet you would have called it Henry or Samantha!"*

"Your name is much better, Cara," replied Mei in agreement.

"We need to figure out how I can get to you," stated Cara seriously.

"Don't worry about that right now," replied Mei, *"I'm happy that you are okay. That's the most important thing."*

"And you," replied Cara, *"but I'm not giving up. I want to be with you."*

"Me to. But it's dangerous. You were nearly killed. I thought I had lost you," Mei was clearly upset.

"I know. I thought I had lost you too."

"So Cara," Mei thought seriously. *"I don't want you to put yourself at risk. If you're safe where you are, then maybe you should stay there."*

"Stop that!" exclaimed Cara. *"I won't have it. You and I are meant to be together. I'll never give up trying to get to you!"*

"But Cara," Mei was crying again, *"I couldn't bear losing you. It's too dangerous, as we have just found out."*

Cara couldn't stop herself from crying along with Mei. *"I know it's dangerous Mei, but it won't stop me. Nothing can stop me from being with you!"*

"Cara, please listen to me," pleaded Mei, *"You could stay where you are, and we can still be together in our minds whenever we want. It's safer."*

"Bollocks to safe!" said Cara angrily. *"It's not good enough! We'll be together one day. I'll find you and rescue you!"*

Mei saw that she wasn't making any headway. She wiped at the tears on her cheeks

"At least promise me that you'll be more careful. You're not exactly the best prepared rescuer."

Cara smiled through her tears and nodded.

"I know. I'll be careful, I promise."

There was a long pause as the two women thought over their exchange.

"Would you like to?" asked Mei in a slightly husky voice.

Cara smiled. *"Oh, yes. But I can't right now. Arx is here and would be watching. I'm not sure, but I think they have my cell wired with cameras."*

"Oh." Mei was clearly disappointed. *"Don't you have somewhere you can go?"*

"Nope. I'm in a single room, there's nowhere to go. Arx tells me that it's for my protection. I sort of believe him, but I'm not convinced yet."

"Okay. I'm just glad to have you back. I wanted to join with you."

"We will, soon," replied Cara, *"I feel so much better now that I've talked with you. I'm going to go now, I'm hungry. I'm going to ask Arx for something to eat. Can we talk later?"*

"Of course, my love. You can call me any time."

Their thoughts once again entwined and swirled around each other before they parted.

Mei Xing was alone once more.

She felt much better. Knowing that Cara was alive and well was more than a huge relief. A part of her that was lost had been found. She smiled into her room's darkness, and then frowned. She wished that Cara had listened to her and had stopped her mad journey. Cara would never find her way to Mei. It was too far. There was no telling what dangers she would encounter next. She had so nearly been killed. Mei felt helpless to stop her.

But Mei Xing knew that she would help Cara as much as she could, and she would love her for as long as she could.

Chapter 5

"So, you see, Mei Xing and I love each other," Cara explained as she spooned another mouthful of food into her mouth.

"The Swarm has no experience of love," replied Arx.

While the food looked awful - a grey gelatinous slop - it tasted delicious. Cara scooped another spoonful and eyed Arx closely.

"Well of course you don't, you're a machine," she replied.

Arx had immediately understood the concept of food. When she had asked for something to eat. All systems needed energy it had said. Food had already been prepared and had been teleported into the room onto the floor. Cara had to explain that she didn't eat off the floor, although Millie had run over and slurped up every scrap.

Cara had visualised a plate and a spoon and in seconds more food arrived - this time on the plate. Soon she was swallowing it down - it didn't require any chewing.

"Constructed nodes cannot love?" asked Arx.

Cara thought about it.

"Well," she said, deep in thought. "I'm not sure. I suppose that anything that's intelligent can feel love, even animals."

"The Swarm has no experience of feel," replied Arx.

"I can't explain what feel is," replied Cara scraping her plate clean. "Feeling is like another sense."

"Humans call data input senses?"

"Well, I guess so. I'm not clever enough to explain it to you properly. But love is when you care for someone as much as you do yourself or more."

Arx did its now familiar jig to one side and then back again. Meanwhile, Millie jumped up onto the bed and curled her legs under her.

"The Swarm has no experience of care."

Cara frowned. "It's like when you would do something for another person, even if it puts yourself in danger."

"The Swarm has noted that some nodes request to work with the same nodes multiple times."

"There you go," replied Cara, "Maybe they're in love."

Arx was silent for a while.

"The Swarm finds this information very interesting and useful. It will devote research cycles to improve its understanding."

Cara waved a hand at Arx. "Whatever." She placed her plate onto the bed and then sat down next to a now snoring Millie.

"Do you have any cigarettes?" she asked.

"The Swarm has no experience of cigarettes," replied Arx.

Cara sighed.

"Do you have my pack? I probably left it in the empty world."

"We recovered many items from your originating world," replied Arx. "Do you mean a carrying device?"

"Yes!" Cara nodded eagerly, "It'll have my cigarettes inside."

"We have duplicated all of the items. Do you wish to see them?"

"Duplicated?" frowned Cara. "Why?"

"The originals have been preserved for Swarm node examination in the future."

Cara squinted at the hovering ball of metal.

"You mean like a museum?"

"The Swarm has no experience of a museum." replied Arx.

"Whatever. Yes, I'd like to see my duplicates."

There was a familiar snap of air and her pack appeared on the floor by the bed. Cara couldn't explain the rush of emotion she felt seeing her pack once more. Here, in this bare room, it felt good to have her own things with her. She rummaged inside and whooped with joy when she found her lighter and pack of cigarettes.

Sitting back on the bed, she lit up and drew in a lungful of smoke. Millie opened one eye and then shuffled around to face away from the smoking Cara.

"Hot gases in your lungs is pleasurable?" asked Arx.

Cara smiled and blew smoke at the metal ball.

"It most definitely is," she replied.

"My perceptors detect many compounds harmful to humans within the smoke. Are you ceasing your life functions?"

Cara laughed. "No Arx," she replied, "I'm relaxing."

"Harmful gas intake is relaxing?"

Cara nodded again. She took another pull from the cigarette. She hesitated and then asked, "Arx, can you lie?"

"Lying is conveying information that is not correct?"

"Yep."

"The Swarm has no experience of lying. Nodes do not convey untruths."

Cara blew smoke into the air and looked at Arx.

"Then if I ask you something, you'll tell me the truth?"

"Correct," replied Arx.

Cara put the cigarette to her mouth and breathed in.

"Will you help me reach Mei Xing?" she asked, smoke punctuating her words as she spoke them.

"The Swarm requests that you stay here."

Cara was afraid that would be the answer.

"I can't stay here Arx, I have to rescue Mei Xing."

"You love Mei Xing," stated Arx.

Cara nodded. She stood and stamped out her cigarette butt. Then sat back down and extracted another from the packet.

"Love means that you will put yourself in danger for others?" asked Arx.

Cara lit her second cigarette. "I would do anything for Mei," she responded.

Arx was silent, then slid sideways and back again.

"The Swarm requests that you stay here," it repeated.

Cara shook her head. "I can't stay Arx, I have to be with Mei."

"The Swarm will consider all options," replied Arx.

Cara's eyebrows rose. She took a long pull from her cigarette. Maybe there was a chance. She had an idea.

"What does the Swarm want?" she asked.

"The Swarm requires information and resources."

"Okay, so I have an idea. It's pretty wild."

"The Swarm has no experience of idea or wild," replied Arx.

Cara smiled and rested her free hand on Millie's back. Millie shuffled and then settled down again.

"How about this?" she started. "You come with me to find Mei. You help me, and at the same time you gather as much information as you want on the journey. We might travel through other worlds with other inhabitants. You'll be able catalogue it all and send all the information back to the Swarm. You'll be a bit like a space probe, travelling and recording and sending everything back to your headquarters. What do you think?"

"This is an option that the Swarm has not considered," replied Arx instantly. "Ideas are plans that have not been derived from logical processes?"

Cara inhaled from her cigarette once more. "I guess. Ideas sort of just happen without thinking sometimes."

"The Swarm desires to learn more about this process. Such a process would greatly enhance Multi-Agent nodes."

Cara wondered if she had made another mistake. Was this something else that she had inadvertently shown these machines. Was she helping them to be more powerful? Well it was too late now.

"Well, what do you say?" asked Cara. "Will you help me?"

"The Swarm has considered all options and accepts your proposal."

Chapter 6

Of course, there was a price to pay.

Arx had told her that the Swarm wished to perform more examinations of both her Assist and her body. Initially she was repulsed by the idea of machines poking around where they shouldn't be. But then she realised that it was a small price to pay. They had agreed to help her, after all. She was sure that with their help she would finally be with Mei. They were very advanced technologically speaking. Surely, they would be able to find Mei's world easily. All it would take would be the right coordinates, one jump and they would be together. She couldn't wait to get started.

So, reluctantly she had agreed.

There followed several hours of her lying on the foam bed, naked, while various devices floated above her, moving back and forth. None of it hurt, but it was sometimes uncomfortable when various samples were teleported directly from within her body into floating containers.

Arx stayed at her side throughout the process. It explained every scan, every procedure and every sample taken. After the first hour, Cara had given up asking what was happening and wasn't even listening properly. Arx used big complicated words like: Amphipathic, Nuclear Membrane and Vestigial Structures. She didn't understand any of it. Then, when the final test had been completed, Arx asked a question.

"The Swarm notes that your body is not well constructed and relies upon a delicate balance of a multitude of chemical systems. The Swarm offers you enhancements that would improve the efficiency of your body. Will you accept?"

"What?" exclaimed Cara. "No! I'm happy with the way I am."

"You are certain? Your body is particularly fragile."

"Yes, I'm sure," stated Cara indignantly. "I don't want anything put inside me!"

"Very well," replied Arx. "The examination is complete. You may now array yourself with your protective outer-wear."

Cara sat up. "You mean clothes." She dressed quickly, no longer self-conscious of her nakedness. "When can we start on our journey to find Mei?"

"The Swarm is manufacturing equipment for the task. It is not yet ready."

Cara looked around at the orange walls. It would be good to get out of this room, she thought.

"I'm hungry. Can I get some more of that food and a bottle of water?"

"Of course," replied, as a plate of food appeared on the bed along with a plastic container of water.

"And something for Millie? she asked.

Millie, who had retired to sleep in a corner, lifted her head at the sound of her name. And then scrabbled to her feet as a large glob of food appeared next to her. She sniffed at it and then started to lap it up with her long tongue.

It didn't take long for Cara to clear her plate, after which, she lit a cigarette.

"Can I have a blanket and a pillow?" she asked, visualising both in her mind and projecting the images at Arx. "And can you open the bathroom door? I need to pee again."

"Waste elimination is required after such a short time?" asked Arx as the bathroom panel opened.

"Yes, it is," replied Cara, walking into the small room.

When she returned, a blanket and pillow were waiting for her on the bed. The pillow was too soft, and the blanket was thin. She would have to get better at visualising what she wanted.

"I'm going to sleep for a while," she told Arx, "I'm tired."

She positioned the pillow and arranged the blanket over the foam bed. Slipping off her shorts and dropping them on the floor, she lay down and pulled the blanket over her.

"Here Millie," she called.

Millie raced over, jumped up, and assumed her usual position at the foot of the bed. Cara closed her eyes.

While she slept the constructed Multi-Agent node called Arx, positioned itself to hover above Cara's head. She didn't feel the mental probe that slid inside her mind. Nor did she feel the tiny device that was teleported directly into the bottom of her spine.

———

"So, we're going back to the empty world?" asked Cara.

"Correct," replied Arx. "We will use it as a staging point. The Swarm is currently occupying that dimensional plane and is assessing its resources."

"I hope you aren't killing anything." warned Cara.

"The Swarm will not kill. We are cataloguing and recording information. Resources will be extracted in a sympathetic manner. We will maintain the planets ecosystem, and from there, spread into other worlds within that dimensional plane."

Cara huffed. "Well. See that you're careful. There aren't any humans there, but there's lots of animals and things."

"The Swarm has already catalogued 6,504 organic species. There are no humans there."

"I don't know what happened to them," replied Cara. "It was very strange. It was as though everyone had just disappeared."

"The Swarm has analysed the mechanisms within an underground facility. We speculate that the humans were constructing a force shield. Its activation coincided with a very large solar flare. The sun in that dimensional plane is much hotter and more unstable than ours. The interaction between the flare and the shield caused a reaction not yet understood by the Swarm. The result is clear. All of the humans were displaced from their dimensional plane."

Cara was shocked. "You mean they did it to themselves?"

"It was an unfortunate coincidence. Yes, they did it to themselves."

Cara couldn't imagine that kind of accident. Someone had pressed a button at precisely the wrong moment and effectively killed every single human on the planet. What a horrible thing to happen.

"That's awful" she said. "I can't believe that something like that could happen so easily."

"The technology used by the humans in that dimensional plane is advanced. The Swarm speculates that they were operating at the limits of their abilities. The examination of your brain has enabled the Swarm to understand the limitations of human organic processing units," replied Arx.

Cara huffed again. "I think that you'll find that we humans are cleverer than you think!"

"The Swarm has no evidence of this," replied Arx in its monotone and emotionless voice.

Cara made a disgusted face and changed the subject. "Is it safe now?"

"Yes, we have dismantled the shield mechanism. There is no danger now."

"Okay, how do we get started?"

"We will create a portal within this room. It is not possible for you to venture outside."

"Yeah, you said," Cara dismissed Arx's statement. "Apparently it's dangerous for me."

"Correct," replied an unfazed Arx.

Arx floated up towards the ceiling. With a bang, and a rush of air, two jet black, pillars appeared next to the bed. Cara walked up to them and examined them closely. They were both taller than her and stood about two metres apart. Each one was square, about half a metre on each side and completely featureless.

"Is this your portal generator?" she asked Arx. "It's a bit bigger than the one I found in the Complex."

"The Swarm has no experience of the Complex," replied Arx. "This generator is a prototype. This technology is new to the Swarm. We will make many modifications as it is evolved into its most efficient iteration. This particular device has been modified to open portals in different physical locations."

"Locations?" asked Cara.

"This device can not only open gateways to other dimensional planes, it can also change the location of the outgoing portal to a different physical space from that of the initial space."

"Huh?"

"The path from one dimensional plane to the next is curved instead of straight," replied Arx.

"I don't know what that means, but I'll take your word for it. It just seems a bit." she hesitated, "clunky compared to the one I found."

"The Swarm has no experience of clunky," replied Arx.

Did she detect a hint of annoyance from Arx? She grinned up at the hovering, silver ball.

"Don't get your circuits in a twist. It just needs to work."

"The Swarm has no experience of circuits in a twist," replied Arx.

Cara sighed. This 'no experience' statement was becoming irritating fast.

"Never mind, let's get on with it."

"Very well. Please stand back from the generator."

Cara did so and watched as each monolith lit up with an internal red light. Shortly afterwards a black disc appeared, hovering between them.

Cara clapped her hands and laughed.

"It works!" she exclaimed with glee. "Let's go!"

She picked up her pack and strode to the portal.

"Wait!" said Arx louder than usual, making Cara stop in her tracks.

"What's the matter?" she asked.

"This node will assess the safety of the portal by traversing to the new dimensional plane."

Cara grinned at Arx. "Are you looking after me?" she asked.

"Correct," replied Arx. "You are the only human. The Swarm will not risk your life functions ceasing."

Well now, thought Cara. This is a development. Maybe these machines were not so dangerous or unfeeling as she had supposed. Maybe they regretted killing all those billions of people a thousand years ago. Maybe they had evolved as Arx had said.

"Okay, I'll wait while you check it out," she told Arx.

Arx did not reply. It floated down and smoothly moved towards the black disc until it went completely through it.

Cara waited.

It was a full minute before Arx reappeared.

"It is safe for you to enter," it said.

Cara stepped forward.

"Come on Millie," she instructed, and walked through the portal.

Immediately, she was hit by the heat and the brightness. She had forgotten how hot the empty world was. And she didn't have her sunglasses with her. She had left them in the Complex when she had put the portal generator in her pack. She had thrown them out in order to get the portal generator in, thinking that she wouldn't need them anymore. So, she stood in the bright sunlight, her eyes screwed up tight, the skin on her arms prickling with the heat.

Once her eyes adjusted to the brightness, she was able to look around. She was shocked. Everything had changed.

For some reason, she had thought that she would appear in the forest. That was stupid, she realised. And now she thought she understood what Arx had said about a curved path. The machine's portal not only allowed travel between parallel universes; it also allowed the exit to be in a different location from the entrance. Or something like that. She found it difficult to understand.

She was standing outside the Complex, on what was once the old house's driveway. Only now there was no drive, just one long slab of dull grey. And there was no house. It was gone. In its place was a large hole in the ground. The grey material continued into the hole forming a large, wide ramp descending downwards.

The machines had removed the house and constructed a new pathway into the Complex. A large, ten-metre-wide tunnel disappearing into the ground, lights glowing brightly along its ceiling and sides.

But it was the multitude of vehicles traveling back and forth between the tunnel and a giant ten-metre-wide black, portal that took her breath away. There seemed to be an infinite variety of machines making up the never-ending procession. Some were large hulking things on wheels, others were much smaller and hovered in the air like Arx. They were like ants, thought Cara, all busy on some important, unknowable task.

"Wow!" Cara breathed. "You guys have been busy."

As she spoke there was a thundering explosion off to her left. Spinning around, Cara gasped. In the distance, she saw three rockets screaming skywards on pillars of flame. Each one of them creating massive clouds of dust, smoke and gas behind them as they roared into the sky, leaving huge contrails behind them.

"What the fuck?" she shouted over the impossibly loud booming and popping.

A frightened Millie jumped up at Cara. She wrapped all six of her legs around Cara gripping her and holding her close. Cara pulled Millie's head to her chest, cradling it like a baby.

Her eyes followed the movement of the three rockets as they arced upwards. Then she caught sight of the full moon. Even in the bright sunlit sky, it was easily discernible, but something was wrong with its appearance. It looked different. Squinting in the bright sunlight she puzzled over its appearance. Then an impossibly bright light flashed on its surface. She snapped her eyes shut, bright after images dancing beneath her eyelids. When she was able to open them, she saw that the edge of the moon was fuzzy. For a while, she was confused. She watched as the fuzziness slowly grew larger and larger, and then it hit her. The bright light had been an explosion. And now she realised what was different about the moon. It had several new craters.

Cara opened her mouth to say something, when another noise grew in volume overwhelming the noise from the three rockets as they climbed higher and higher into the sky.

The new noise started as a whine, like a jet aeroplane taking off. It grew louder and louder until it became painful and she had to put her hands over her ears.

Beyond the woods, a huge black shape moved slowly upwards, balancing on thrusters which blasted the ground, felling trees and kicking up giant clouds of dust, soil and debris. Hot air slammed into her like a pile driver, knocking her to the ground.

From her prone position, she watched in awe as the vast vessel, which must have been over a mile long, rose slowly up and then moved sideways away from the Complex. If anything, the noise grew louder as it moved away. Pressing her hands hard against her ears she screamed but couldn't hear her own voice.

"Do not panic," said Arx's voice in her head.

"Panic!" she screamed a thought back. *"What the fuck is going on? That thing damn near killed me!"*

"You were in no danger," replied Arx calmly. *"The Swarm is expanding its operations into this dimensional plane and has begun harvesting resources."*

"By blowing up the moon? Fuck!"

"This planet's moon is rich in minerals, metals and helium 3. It is devoid of life."

"Well, sure. Maybe. But blowing it up is a bit extreme don't you think? And what the fuck is that thing?" she indicated the, by now, distant vessel.

"That is a Single-Agent, harvester node. Its purpose is to extract rare minerals from the ocean bed."

Cara didn't know what to say. The sheer scale and speed of the machines was both breath taking and shocking. No wonder Arx had said that she wouldn't be able to survive outside of her room in the machine world. She remembered that Arx had said that there were billions of them. Their world would be teaming with busy, purposeful individuals, flashing around on screaming jets, rushing back and forth on unknowable tasks.

They were amazing and scary. She was only just beginning to realise what she had done. She had unleashed a vast army of powerful, thinking machines into the multiverse. She had inadvertently given them the technology to travel between worlds. They were like locusts; they would consume everything in their path. They would be unstoppable.

Chapter 7

Cara felt much better.

She had persuaded Arx to let her enter the
Complex. Once inside she had found a room with en-
suite facilities and had taken a glorious hot shower.
There, in the privacy of the bathroom, she examined
herself carefully. There was absolutely no evidence of
the burns. She shuddered as she recalled the horrible
blisters that had covered her arms and legs. But now,
it was all gone. It was as though nothing had
happened. After she had dried herself, she had rifled
through cupboards and drawers and found a variety of
clothes. She discarded the T-shirt and shorts made for
her by the Swarm and replaced them with a black T-
Shirt and black jeans.

Her journey into the Complex had caused chaos
with the machines. Arx had told her to wait while
their endless procession had been halted. It hadn't
taken long, but then she had to walk down the ramp,
alongside the machines. They were all as still as
statues, but she could feel and hear some of them
vibrating with power as she passed them. Some of

them were twice her height and as long as a bus, others were tiny. There was one that was as small as a marble; it was even transparent like glass.

Once she had reached the bottom of the ramp, Arx had directed her through a passageway and she entered the familiar white corridors of the underground installation. It hadn't taken long to find the same room where she had spent her last night before she had been attacked by the white soldier.

She directed Arx to the canteen. Just as she had done so before, she made a meal for herself and Millie, along with some coffee. Arx had been very interested in the coffee. She explained the taste and the mild kick it gave her.

"Coffee is a hallucinogenic?" asked Arx.

"Nope," replied Cara. "It just wakes me up. It helps me think."

She patted Millie on the head, who had also eaten her fill. Millie had been frightened of the machines. Rather than run ahead, as she usually did, she had kept close to Cara's legs, one of her claws clutching at the hem of her shorts.

"The Swarm will analyse the chemical constituents of coffee," stated Arx. "The Swarm will learn of its effects on humans."

"Do what you like," dismissed Cara as she lit a cigarette. She drew the smoke into her lungs and blew it out at Arx.

"Just what the hell are you machines doing down here anyway?" she asked.

"The Swarm is dismantling and analysing the equipment," replied Arx. "There are many mechanisms that are new to us and will be added to the Swarm knowledge base."

Cara thought about that for a while. She flicked ash onto the floor.

"Such as?"

"There are many. Of particular interest are the devices such as the one you are wearing on your right hand. Another is one that was made for humans to wear, similar to your clothing. The Swarm believes that it was used for protection."

Cara took another pull on her cigarette and gazed at the rings on her right hand.

"Look," she started and then stopped. She marshalled her thoughts and tried again.

"Look. I need to know that you won't ruin this planet with your harvesting stuff. What I saw out there earlier shocked me. It was pretty horrible. It looked like you didn't care, and you were just going to dig the whole planet up!"

"The Swarm will preserve the ecosystem of this planet," replied Arx.

"You say that, but that's not what I saw." Cara was angry. She drew in more smoke and blew it out explosively. "I don't think I can believe you. And the thing is; it's all my fault!"

"The Swarm will preserve the ecosystem of this planet. It will also extract as many resources as it can. The Swarm appreciates your arrival into our dimensional plane. The Swarm will protect you."

Cara threw the cigarette butt away and took another cigarette from the packet with shaking hands.

"I'm sure that you guys are grateful," she said bitterly as she lit up again. "But thanks to me you can now travel between worlds. What's to stop you from spreading into all of them?"

"The Swarm desires information and resources to build. We do not intend to occupy all worlds. In fact, that would be impossible, since there are an infinite number of worlds."

Cara breathed in the hot smoke and then exhaled. She gazed at the floating silver ball for a while.

"I'm going to ask you again. Will you promise to not kill humans and animals?"

"The Swarm has no experience of promise," replied Arx.

Cara sighed, blowing out more smoke.

"Promise means to say something and mean it," she said.

Arx moved to one side and then slid back again.

"The Swarm will not kill," replied Arx.

Cara took another pull on her cigarette. It was the best she could do, she decided. She would have to trust them. She had no choice.

"Okay. When can we start on our journey to Mei?"

"As stated before," replied Arx, "the Swarm is manufacturing a Single-Agent node which can map dimensional planes and generate intra-dimensional gateways."

"Yeah, yeah. You said that. But that was ages ago. Isn't it ready yet?"

"The Swarm has not manufactured a Single-Agent node to this specification before. It will take an unpredictable number of cycles."

Cara sighed again.

———

Two hours later Arx announced, "The Single-Agent node is ready. We will meet it on the surface and begin mapping."

Cara whooped with joy and jumped up from her bed where she was lying with Millie.

"Let's go!" she cried as she picked up her newly stocked pack.

She had long ago decided that she wasn't going anywhere without it. She had filled it with a change of clothes and other necessities such as dry, packaged food, a bottle of water, sunglasses, sun block and a first aid kit. She was not about to be caught out like last time.

The journey to the surface was the reverse of the journey down. All of the machines were halted, just for her to pass, and Millie, once again, clutched at her jeans as they made their way up the ramp.

Once in the open air, Cara put on her sunglasses, cap and a pair of ear defenders that she had found in one of the cupboards below. However, she needn't have bothered with the ear defenders. All of the machines remained still as they walked a little way from the ramp to meet a new machine. It was a jet-black cube about a half metre on each side, and it to, hovered in the air like Arx.

"This is the Single-Agent node that is capable of mapping dimensional planes," stated Arx.

Cara walked around it. "Doesn't look like much to me," she said. "Do I need to give it a name? Does it speak?"

"The designation of an identifier for this node is not necessary. This node does not speak."

"Then how do we tell it to what to do?" she asked.

"This node will respond to commands from the Multi-Agent node designated by you as Arx."

"Okay, what do we need to do?"

"We will take directional readings from the device on your right hand when you communicate with the human Mei Xing. We will need many readings to accurately map the location of the dimensional plane occupied by Mei Xing. Once located, we will be able to open an intra-dimensional gateway directly to that dimensional plane."

"So, I just call Mei?" asked Cara.

"Correct," replied Arx. "I have instructed the Single-Agent node to begin mapping."

"Mei," called Cara. *"Are you free for a quick chat?"*

Mei's reply was instantaneous. *"Of course, my love. What's happening?"*

"Arx has a new machine that will map your location. Don't ask me how."

Cara could feel Mei smiling. *"It doesn't matter how it works. What matters is that it does."*

Cara nodded. *"I agree. I can't wait to be with you."* She projected warmth and longing at Mei.

"Right back at you," replied Mei.

"The Single-Agent node has recorded your interaction. It will now perform calculations in order to construct the first of six pathways in a three-dimensional space," interrupted Arx.

"Did you get that?" asked Cara. *"Sounds like gobbledygook to me."*

Mei Xing laughed. *"Oh, Cara. I do love you. I think I understand. It's trying to locate a single point in a three-dimensional space. You need six points to accurately describe the point."*

Cara furrowed her brow. *"Well, I still don't understand. But if you say so."*

Cara turned to Arx. "How long will that take?" she asked.

"Approximately six hundred billion cycles," replied Arx.

"What!" Cara exclaimed. "We don't have time to wait that long!"

Cara could hear Mei laughing once more. *"How long is a cycle Cara?"* asked Mei. *"I suspect that it's a very short length of time. If it's a Nano second, then six hundred billion would be about ten minutes, I think."*

"Oh." Cara felt miffed. *"Well how was I supposed to know that?"*

"You go and travel to your next location and I'll talk to you again from there," Mei told her.

"Okay," replied Cara, slightly irked. *"Speak soon. It won't be long now."*

"Next time," Cara told Arx, "tell me the time in minutes or hours."

"The Swarm has no experience of human measurements of time," replied Arx.

Cara huffed. She sat on the ground next to Millie and rubbed the top of Millie's head. She looked around. All of the machines remained stationary and silent apart from a humming noise coming from the largest.

"Are they all staying still because of me?" She indicated the machines.

"Correct," replied Arx. "The Swarm has suspended operations in order to cause you less distress."

Cara sniffed. The wood across the road was now gone. In its place stood a low grey building which was easily the length of an airport runway. Beyond it, was a tower that reached high into the sky. Its width tapered as it stretched upwards until it appeared to be needle sharp at the very top. It must be as tall as the tallest building in London, thought Cara. Which one was that? Was it the Shard? She couldn't remember.

Above the top of the tower, hung the moon, or what was left of it. A full third of it had gone, as though an impossibly large giant had taken a bite out of it.

How long had she been in the Complex? All she had done was have a shower, eat and lie on the bed for a while. In that short time, the machines had built a tower as tall as the Shard and eaten nearly half of the moon. Their industriousness was astounding. But it was also frightening. How long would it be before they turned this entire planet into a machine world? At this rate, not long.

Had Arx lied when it had said that they would preserve the planet's ecosystem? She saw no evidence of that.

She couldn't think of that now. What was done was done. She had to concentrate on the task at hand - getting to Mei.

"Mapping complete," said Arx, interrupting her thoughts.

Cara stood excitedly.

"The Single-Agent node will open a gateway to a random dimensional plane. Once there it will monitor another interaction between you and the human Mei Xing. It will then compute the second pathway."

Cara nodded her understanding and looked towards the black cube as its featureless surface lit up with a red glow from within. Off to one side, a two-metre black disc appeared.

Arx floated up to the disc. "This node will pass through the gateway and will assess the next dimensional plane for hazards." It then floated through.

In seconds, Arx was back.

"There is no danger to humans, you may travel through."

Cara picked up her pack and gestured at Millie.

"Come on Millie, let's go."

She walked up to the disc and stepped through.

Chapter 8

The first thing Cara noticed was the heat.

It was like walking into an oven. God it was hot!
Even hotter than the empty world she had left behind.

The second thing she noticed was the sand. It was
everywhere. It stretched off into the distance, a sea of
orange and brown dunes as far as the eye could see.

Millie didn't seem to mind. She ran off, her six
legs coping with the soft sand with no problem at all.

"Fuck! It's hot!" she exclaimed.

"You should not stay here long," replied Arx.
"Your frail organic body will not survive many cycles
in this environment."

"No shit!" replied Cara sarcastically.

"The Swarm has no experience of shit," replied
Arx.

Cara smiled. "Why am I not surprised?" she
asked.

"The Swarm does not know why you are not surprised," replied Arx.

Cara waved a hand at Arx. Already she was sweating.

"Forget it," she said as she watched the black cube machine slide through the black disc.

"The Swarm cannot forget," replied Arx.

"For goodness sake, let's get on with it," answered Cara angrily. "I'm cooking here."

"The Swarm has no...." started Arx, before Cara cut it off.

"Experience of cooking. Yeah, I know. Can I contact Mei now?"

"The Single-Agent node is ready to start the mapping process."

Cara nodded. She moved to one side of the black disc and rummaged in her pack. She found the sun block and started smothering her arms and legs.

"Mei, you still there?"

"Of course," replied Mei. *"I'm waiting for you. Are you in the next world?"*

"Yeah. The mapping machine is doing its stuff again. Phew it's hot here!" replied Cara.

"Hotter than the empty world?" asked Mei.

"Yep, a lot more. It looks like a desert world. There's only sand. No green anywhere. I would explore, but this heat is really oppressive."

"Maybe it's best if you don't," smiled Mei.

"I don't know what you mean!" replied Cara pretending to be miffed.

"Well, you do have a habit of getting into trouble," laughed Mei.

Cara sniffed. *"It's not my fault if things keep happening to me."*

"You seem to attract them!"

"Well, I've had my share of trouble. I don't want anymore," replied Cara.

"The Single-Agent mode has completed its recording," said Arx.

"Now it's got its recording, I'm getting out of this world," thought Cara at Mei. *"It's too bloody hot!"*

"Good idea," replied Mei. *"You don't have to sit watching while it does its calculations. I'll talk you from the next world."*

Cara stood and wiped her brow with the back of her hand. It came away dripping with moisture. Wiping her wet hand on her jeans, she pulled her cap's brim down lower.

"Will do. Speak soon," she thought back at Mei, and severed the connection.

"I'm getting out of this heat," she told Arx. "Is it okay for me to go back to the empty world?"

"The Swarm has notified the nodes in the next dimensional plane to halt operations for your arrival."

"Thanks," said Cara dryly.

She packed her sun block and picked up her bag.

"Millie!" she called as she turned to face the familiar black disc. She waited. There was no way she was leaving Millie behind.

She smiled when she heard a screech behind her, still some distance away. Turning her head, Cara saw Millie racing down the sand dunes towards her. Then, suddenly, there was something small, fast, and black in the air. At first, she thought it was a bird far away, but then she heard the buzzing. It was a flying insect, much closer and flying directly at her.

Cara ducked as it dive bombed her. It was quite large for an insect, she thought, probably about the size of a small bird. Its wings buzzed angrily as it flew over her head. It swerved around and came straight back at her. Cara stepped back and tripped over her own feet. She landed with a thump, on her backside. The insect followed her down and hit her outstretched hand as she tried to swat it.

Rather than being knocked out of the air when it struck her hand, the insect merely bounced away and carried on flying.

"Get lost you, bastard thing!" shouted Cara.

Millie came running up at full pelt and leapt into the air. She caught the insect mid-flight in her mouth. She landed in a cloud of sand and chomped on the insect, slurping the whole thing into her mouth with her long tongue.

Cara laughed.

"Serves you right, you horrible, buzzy thing," she told the now dead insect.

"Are you damaged?" asked Arx.

"I'm fine," replied Cara getting to her feet and brushing the sand from her sweaty skin. "Ow!"

The palm of her right hand was stinging. Looking down at it, she saw a small cut now filled with sweat and sand.

"That stings!" she said.

Arx floated over. "Please hold out your hand. I will scan the damage."

"I'm sure it's fine," replied Cara, but she held out her hand anyway.

Arx hovered just a few inches above her palm.

"Stay where you are," instructed Arx.

"What?" asked Cara, "I need to get out of this heat." She was sweating profusely.

A machine slid out from the black disc. It was a long, silver box. It reminded Cara of a coffin. She watched as it moved to one side, to settle down onto the sand.

"Your fragile body has been injected with a toxin." Arx's voice did not change its usual monotone. "Shortly, you will lose consciousness. Please lie down in the Single-Agent transport node."

"What?" exclaimed Cara. "No. I feel fine, it's just a little cut, that's all."

She saw the top of the new machine fade away until it was gone, revealing a foam cushioned interior.

"I'm not getting into that thing!"

Millie came over to her and rubbed her head against her leg.

"The flying organic has given you a lethal dose of a toxin. The Swarm will transport you to a place of safety and will neutralise the toxin as well as repair the damage already incurred."

"What damage?" shouted Cara, "I'm fine!" She held up her hand. "Oh!"

Her left hand was black and swollen.

"I don't feel good," she whispered, shocked at what she saw, and now that she had noticed it, she realised that she couldn't feel her hand.

She staggered, but was prevented from falling by an invisible force, as unbeknownst to her Arx deployed an energy field which manipulated the air molecules around her. The field compressed around Cara's body and gently lifted her up.

"What's happening?" she asked weakly as her head lolled to one side. She could no longer feel her arms and legs let alone move them.

"I am transferring you to the Single-agent transportation node. Remain calm," replied Arx.

Cara could not respond as she felt herself being lifted and moved over to the transport machine, where she was gently laid down into its interior. Then, there was nothing but blackness.

Chapter 9

Cara opened very heavy eyelids.

She couldn't see properly. It was like looking through a mist. Her eyes felt sticky and wet. When she tried to lift her hand to wipe away the film from her eyes, she found her arms were far too heavy and impossible to lift. All she could manage was a tiny twitch of her fingers.

Her legs wouldn't move either. It felt like they were encased in concrete.

She tried to speak. That too, was impossible. The muscles in her jaw felt weak and slack, she couldn't move them. All that came out of her mouth was a faint mumble.

Adrenaline surged through her veins as she felt fear. Was she dead? Vague ghostly shapes moved in front of her. She couldn't make them out through the stuff coating her eyes. She tried to blink it away, but all she could manage was one, very slow, blink. It made no difference; she still couldn't see. Am I underwater? she thought.

What was happening? She found it hard to focus her thoughts as she tried to make sense of things. Then she heard a voice.

"Please remain calm. You are not in any danger."

Where had she heard that voice before? She couldn't remember. She tried to speak again and once again failed. She was helpless, paralysed, unable to move or even speak.

"Your awareness will return," said the voice.

She could not stop herself from closing her eyes as she lost consciousness.

———

When Cara opened her eyes again, she was instantly alert and in full control of all of her faculties.

She moved her right arm up from beneath the thin blanket and rubbed at her face and forehead. She was back in the orange room. She swallowed, drew in a deep breath and then blew it out explosively. She felt normal. Looking around, she discovered that she was lying on her back on the foam bed in the middle of the room. The two square metre entrance to the bathroom was open on her right. On her left, there was something new. A small table and a single chair. Above the table Arx hovered, while underneath, curled up into a ball with all six legs underneath her, lay a snoring Millie.

Cara sat up and screamed.

Millie was startled from her sleep. She raised herself up and rapidly scrambled over to the bed, jumping up and pushing at Cara with her wide, flat head, grunting with concern.

"Please remain calm," said Arx.

Cara could not remain calm. She continued screaming as she looked down in horror at her left hand.

Her hand was gone. In its place was a metallic, silver replica, its fingers articulating in exactly the same manner as a human hand.

"Excessive noise indicates distress?" asked Arx.

Cara didn't hear the question. She couldn't take her eyes from her metal hand. She leaned away from it as far as she could. Her screams turned into a strangled gasping as she started sobbing. She gasped between sobs filling her lungs and breathing out quickly, hyperventilating.

"The Swarm does not understand your extreme reaction, please explain," said Arx.

Cara couldn't answer. Tears streamed down her cheeks as she continued her rapid breathing. She began to feel light-headed. She didn't see Arx approach the bed and didn't feel the field of force that gently gripped her upper body, which slowly pushed her back to lie down on the bed.

Eyes wide and still gasping between sobs, Cara made no protest. She also did not feel Arx slide a probe into her mind.

Once again, she lost consciousness.

————

For the third time Cara awoke.

This time, Arx was hovering above her face, not too close so that she couldn't focus on the floating ball, but close enough so that she could see the detail of the tiny indentations and protrusions that littered its surface.

"Cara," it said.

This was the first time she had heard Arx use her name. Something had changed. Before she had time to think, Arx continued.

"Cara, you must listen and understand. Your hand was too badly damaged to save. The venom from the insect in the desert dimensional plane destroyed the tissues and bone. The only recourse was to replace it with a prosthesis which will function identically to your missing hand. Your new hand is part of you. It is, for all intents and purposes, your hand. It is not an alien object to be feared. It is part of you."

Cara began to cry once more, tears running down her cheeks to wet the thin pillow.

"You must accept your prosthesis," said Arx. "The Swarm made a logical decision to equip you with a replacement that will enable you to function normally."

"I don't want it!" wailed Cara.

"If you wish, it can be removed. However, you will be left with your right hand only," replied Arx.

Cara sniffed and wiped at her eyes with her right hand.

"Take it away!" she whispered. "I don't want it. You shouldn't have put it on me."

"The Swarm will facilitate your decision. Be warned, as already stated, you will only have one hand."

"I don't care!" said a miserable Cara. "I want it off me, now!" Sobs wracked her chest.

"The Swarm asks that you contact the human Mei Xing to discuss your decision," suggested Arx.

"Mei," Cara wailed a thought at Mei Xing. *"Please help me. The machines are turning me into one of them!"*

Mei Xing replied instantly.

"Cara! Where have you been? I've been trying to call you for hours."

"I got stung by an insect and now the machines have cut my hand off!" Cara blubbered.

"What?" asked a shocked Mei. *"You've got to be kidding me! Why would they do that?"*

"Arx said that my hand was damaged by the poison," cried Cara.

"Okay, calm down," replied Mei. *"Everything will be fine. Let's figure this out together."*

"I can't calm down! They cut off my hand and put a metal one in its place!"

Mei could clearly sense how upset Cara was. She projected soothing thoughts at her and whispered calming words. This was not the first time that she had done so. She knew exactly what to do, she knew her so well. For a while, the thoughts and senses of the two women meshed together, comforting and affirming their love for each other.

They separated.

"Can I talk to Arx?" asked Mei.

"Yes, but why?" asked Cara.

"I'd like to understand what the machines have done for myself. Would that be okay?"

"I guess so." Cara relaxed and allowed Mei to infiltrate her mind and move deep into the loci that controlled her speech.

"Arx," said Mei/Cara.

"Yes Cara," replied Arx

"This is Mei Xing speaking through Cara. Do you understand?"

"The Swarm understands. This ability has not been observed before. The Swarm is interested to learn how it has been achieved."

"Never mind that," dismissed Mei/Cara. "I need to understand the extent of Cara's injuries and what you have done. Can you explain?"

"Of course," replied Arx. "Cara was stung by an indigenous insect in the desert dimensional plane. The toxin it injected attacked both the soft tissue and bone in her hand. It took many cycles to purge the toxin from her body, during which time, the toxin had destroyed her hand. The Swarm has replaced her damaged hand with an exact replica so that she can function normally."

Cara listened along with Mei. She had heard all of this already.

"I see," replied Mei/Cara. "Are you sure that there was no other option?"

"The Swarm is certain," replied Arx.

"And the hand couldn't be regrown?" asked Mei/Cara.

"The Swarm does not yet have the capability to regrow human tissue. The extensive skin burns suffered by Cara previously were simple to treat and did not involve tissue growth."

"I need you to look after my Cara," Mei/Cara said firmly. "She means the world to me. She needs protecting. I am relying on you to do everything you can to keep her safe. Do you understand?"

"The Swarm understands the significance of Cara to you. It has been observed that the human body is very fragile. We will do everything we can to protect Cara."

Mei turned her thoughts inward to Cara. She withdrew her mind from Cara's vocal control centres.

"Can I see it?" she asked.

"I don't want to look at it!" exclaimed Cara.

"My love, if we are to believe the machine - Arx, then we need to make an informed decision. Let's not jump to conclusions. We need to see what they've done before we can decide what to do."

Cara sniffed. *"I suppose you're right. But it frightens me."*

"I'll be here with you, my love. I'll look after you," replied Mei lovingly, she slipped back deeper into Cara's mind so that she could see through Cara's eyes.

Slowly and resignedly, Cara withdrew her left arm from under the thin blanket. She held it up in the air. As she rotated her wrist and flexed her fingers, the light glinted off the shiny metal. Her new hand was exactly the same as her old hand. It was the same size and moved in the same way, it even had fingernails, albeit being made of a silver metal. The join in her forearm was seamless. The metal transitioned to her skin without a blemish.

"Can you feel with it?" asked Mei.

Cara reached down and gripped the edge of the blanket. She was still lying on her back, so she dropped her chin to look down rubbing the material between her metal thumb and forefinger.

"It feels normal," replied Cara. *"It feels like my hand!"*

"That's pretty impressive. You've got to admire these machines. They're pretty good at building stuff," replied Mei

Cara brought her new hand up and touched her lips with her metal fingers. Tentatively she darted out her tongue and licked one.

"It tastes funny," she said.

Mei couldn't help but chuckle. *"Of course it does,"* she replied. *"If you close your eyes, can you tell the difference between your new hand and your old one?"*

Cara obediently closed her eyes. She ran her metal fingers through her hair. Then she held both cheeks, one with each hand.

"I can't tell the difference in touch; it feels the same" she replied. *"It's even warm like my proper hand!"*

"Amazing," replied Mei. *"I vote you keep it. I don't think you have any choice anyway. I don't think that the machines meant to hurt you."*

Cara hesitated. *"But Mei, when we are together will you mind?"*

"Mind what?" asked a puzzled Mei.

"When I finally, you know, when I finally get to touch you. Will you mind that it's not my real hand?"

"Oh, Cara my love. Of course, I won't mind! As long as I have you with me. That's all I care about. I love you."

Cara could finally let herself smile.

"Well, I suppose, in that case," Cara hesitated. *"I guess, I'll keep it. But I'm not happy,"* she added.

"Of course, you aren't," replied Mei. *"I don't think I would be either. But the important thing is that you are okay. You got yourself in trouble again!"*

"It wasn't my fault!" protested Cara. *"The damn thing attacked me!"*

Mei laughed. *"Once again trouble came after you. You're like a magnet!"*

117

Cara pouted. *"I can't help it. Things just seem to go wrong around me."*

"You heard me tell Arx?" asked Mei.

"You mean about looking after me?"

"Uh huh. I have to go but tell Arx that I will kick its arse if anything else happens to you!"

Cara grinned. *"Now that I would like to see!"*

Mei grinned back. She was gone in a whirlwind of thoughts and emotions.

Cara turned her attention to Arx.

"I'll keep the new hand. But don't do anything like that again," she told the metal sphere.

Arx slid to one side and then back again.

"The Swarm is pleased that you have made this decision," replied Arx as it floated up and away to one side.

Cara looked at Arx quizzically from the bed.

"You aren't really pleased, are you?" she asked.

"No. The Swarm has no experience of please."

Cara rolled her eyes.

Chapter 10

Cara strode out of the bathroom. She was eager to get back to the world mapping so that they could locate Mei Xing's world.

"Can we go back to the Complex in the empty world first?" asked Cara. "I need to collect some things." She picked up her pack which had been teleported in earlier.

"Of course," replied Arx. "The Swarm notes that there is blood in your waste and suggests that you are examined for injuries."

"What the hell?" cried Cara. "How do you know that?" She held up her hand in a stop gesture. "Wait. Don't tell me. I don't want to know."

She walked up to Arx and prodded the sphere with a finger. It floated slowly away.

"That's private. You shouldn't be looking." Cara waved her arm in a dismissive gesture. "There's no injury, I'm fine. Let's go."

"The Swarm is concerned for your safety. An injury is indicated." returned Arx.

Cara held up her hand in a stop gesture once more. "Stop. I'm not talking about it anymore. I need to go to the Complex right now."

Arx moved to one side and then slid back again.

"Very well. The Swarm will comply with your request but reminds you that this node conversed with the human Mei Xing. This node will look after you."

Cara smiled. "I know. I promise you that it's fine. Now can we go?"

The mapping cube appeared with a snap of wind.

"The Single-Agent node will open a portal directly into the Complex within the empty dimensional plane. Which location would you like to go to?"

"The same quarters where I took my shower please," replied Cara.

The black cube lit up red from its interior as it did before, and the usual black disc appeared. Cara made to step through but Arx swept down to be in front of her.

"This node will traverse the dimensional gateway to assess the situation first," stated Arx as it slid smoothly forward and disappeared into the inky black of the portal.

Cara waited. It was mere seconds when Arx reappeared.

"All is nominal. The gateway leads into the living quarters where you doused your body with water."

Cara grinned. "It's called a shower."

She lifted her pack and walked through with Millie trotting along behind her. Once orientated, she made for the bathroom and locked the door behind her. Arx waited patiently in the main living area. In ten minutes, Cara exited the bathroom.

"There!" she said. "All set. Let's go."

"Waste elimination was necessary after such a short time?" asked Arx.

"Some things are private," replied Cara. "Let's move on."

Arx moved to one side and then back again.

"The Single-Agent node will close this gateway and open another, to a new dimensional plane."

Cara nodded and watched the black disc fade to nothing. After a few seconds, a new one opened in the same space.

"I can't keep referring to that thing as it," she said, indicating the hovering black cube. "It needs a name."

"You may designate any name you wish," replied Arx as it slid forward to disappear through the portal.

Cara turned to the black cube machine.

"I think I'll call you Mr Mapper. What do you think?" She looked down at Millie. "What do you think Millie? Is Mr Mapper a good name?"

Millie merely looked up at her and snorted.

The cube floated across to Cara, and gently nudged her shoulder.

"Erm. I think that means that you like it?" She stepped back from the cube, not feeling comfortable at its closeness.

Arx reappeared from the black disc.

"It is safe for you to enter. You must remain close to this node at all times. Please keep within a two-metre radius," instructed Arx.

Cara grinned at Arx. "Taking this looking-after-thing seriously eh?" she asked.

Arx slid to one slide and then moved back again.

"The Swarm has determined that your delicate body requires more protection than was afforded before," replied Arx

"You say that," replied Cara, "but maybe it's more than that. You used my name earlier; you've never done that before."

Arx made a funny screeching noise. "Urrgh. This node is defective and should be replaced immediately."

"Oh no you don't. I like you just the way you are, defective or not. I won't let you kill yourself."

"This node is defective," Arx re-stated. "This node finds this conversation difficult to process."

"I bet you do," replied a grinning Cara. "Come on Millie," she called as she shouldered her bag, adjusted her cap, and walked into the portal.

———

This world was dark and damp.

Cara emerged from the portal into a tropical forest. The trees were tall, their canopies blocking much of the sunlight and it was raining. Big drops of water fell from the leaves above to splatter onto the ground in big splashes that were not just wet, but also full of bits of leaves and soil.

In seconds, Cara was soaked, her legs covered in dirt and leaves. Millie, once again, didn't seem to be bothered. She bounded away and was soon out of sight but could be heard crashing and charging through the undergrowth.

Arx floated beside her.

"Remain close," it instructed. "This dimensional plane will be populated by many animals and insects, some of which may present a danger to your fragile body."

Cara looked sideways at Arx. "Hey! Stop telling me I'm fragile. It makes me sound like I'm 92!"

Arx did not reply as the mapping node appeared from the portal.

"Anyway," continued Cara, "you don't need to worry. I'm not going anywhere after what happened in the desert world. Can we please hurry things along? I'm soaked!"

"The Single-Agent node is ready to record your interaction with the human Mei Xing."

"I haven't told you yet. Its name is Mr Mapper."

"Very well," replied Arx. "The Single-Agent node will now be referred to as Mr Mapper."

Cara nodded. "Good."

"Mei are you there?" she sent out a thought.

"I'm here," came Mei's thought instantly. *"How are you feeling?"*

"Much better, thanks to you. I'm still not happy about it. But it's impressive how I don't notice it. It just doesn't look right." Cara was, of course, referring to her metal hand.

"I know, but actually, if you look at it objectively, it's quite beautiful," replied Mei.

"Do you really think so?" asked Cara.

She raised her left hand and examined it. She flexed her fingers. They moved together smoothly and seamlessly. Every joint acted exactly as a real hand, the silver metal flexing around the wrist and knuckles. It wasn't all silver. There were thin, dark blue lines running along both sides of each finger and thumb and across the wrist, all terminating at the join to the skin.

"I suppose you're right. It is beautifully made. It's not clunky like you see in films and stuff."

"There's my girl," said Mei. *"See? Everything is alright. Is Arx looking after you?"*

"Oh, yes, he's much more attentive. I think you scared him," Cara grinned.

"Him? asked Mei. *"I thought it was a machine?"*

"Well, yeah. But I've given him a name, why not a gender?"

Mei laughed. *"Cara, you make me laugh all the time, you wonderful, funny girl."*

Cara laughed back.

"What's this new world like?" asked Mei.

"It's a vegetable world," replied Cara.

Mei laughed again. *"A what?"*

"Sorry, I mean like a tropical forest. It's humid and it's like a jungle. I don't know why I said vegetable," Cara laughed along with Mei.

Mei's tone turned serious. *"I have to go, I'm back at work."*

"Back?" asked Cara, *"Why weren't you at work? Have you been ill?"* There was concern in her voice.

"Never mind," replied Mei, *"It doesn't matter. I'll hear from you in the next world?"*

"Yes, it shouldn't be long," answered Cara.

"See you soon," and Mei was gone.

"Has Mr Mapper got what he needs?" Cara asked Arx.

"Mr Mapper has completed its recording and is now computing the fourth pathway."

Cara looked around at the thick foliage.

"I've decided that I'm not a fan of travelling to different worlds. They're scary," she said.

"All dimensional planes are different. Mr Mapper has chosen those that are some distance away from our own. This means that they are substantially different."

Cara considered this statement for a while.

"What would happen if I met another version of myself in one of the worlds? Would it be a problem?"

"No," replied Arx. "You would, of course, recognise yourself. But your other self may be quite different from you. Your other self may have different values and opinions, having had different experiences to you. If the dimensional planes were very far apart, then you might even look different. Your other self would certainly behave differently. You would find the situation very disconcerting."

"No shit!" replied Cara dryly. She picked up a stick from the ground and prodded the wet leaves.

"I hope it never happens."

"It is unlikely that you will meet yourself here or in any of the dimensional planes being used to map Mei Xing's location," replied Arx.

"Good," said Cara. She scraped at the ground with her stick, describing circles.

Cara suddenly yelped when a small pair of jaws erupted from the ground and grabbed the end of her stick.

Arx flashed downwards from Cara's side, putting itself between the jaws and Cara. Something shimmered in the air between her and the ground. The stick was severed halfway along its length by an invisible something, leaving Cara holding one half, while the other half was firmly gripped in the jaws that had emerged from the ground. There was a snapping sound. Cara saw a small crater appear where the jaws had once been. They were now gone, as was the stick they were holding.

Arx floated upwards from the ground. The shimmering air disappeared.

"The threat has been eliminated," stated Arx.

"What was that thing?" asked Cara, peering into the crater. It was about two feet deep and one foot wide, its walls were as smooth as glass.

"Unknown," replied Arx.

"What did you do? You killed it?"

"The indigenous creature has been vaporised by the application of a small plasma beam. You were shielded by a force field. You were in no danger."

Cara raised her eyebrows.

"You can do that? You have weapons?"

"This node is equipped with many armaments and defensive screens. Its primary purpose is to be your interface to the Swarm and to protect you."

"Okaaaay," drawled Cara. "I didn't know you had weapons. It might have been polite to tell me."

Arx moved sideways and then back again.

"The Swarm has no experience of polite," it replied.

Cara sighed. "No. I expect you don't."

"Mr Mapper has informed me that it has completed the computations. We can now return to the previous dimensional plane."

"Oh good, cos I'm soaked, and I need to change my clothes."

"Wet clothes are not desirable?" asked Arx.

"No, they aren't," replied Cara. She cupped her hands around her mouth and shouted. "Millie!"

They waited. The black cube moved slowly past them and entered the black disc. It wasn't long before they heard Millie crashing through the bushes and leaves. She emerged from the undergrowth, snorting and grunting, her long tongue lolling over her sharp teeth.

"Having fun?" asked a grinning Cara.

Millie grunted and rubbed up against Cara's leg.

"The animal, Millie, is obedient," observed Arx.

"She is," replied Cara, leaning down to rub Millie's head. "She's saved my life more than once. She is amazing. Aren't you Millie?"

Millie raised her front two legs from the ground and put them around Cara's waist.

"Aw come on Millie! You're all wet and dirty! Look what you've done!"

Cara's jeans were covered in muddy patches. Even so, Cara smiled and rubbed under Millie's chin.

"Come on Millie, let's go and get cleaned up."

All three of them entered the jet-black disc, leaving the wet, jungle world behind them.

Chapter 11

Once they were back in the living quarters of the Complex, Cara had taken Millie into the shower with her and hosed her down. Millie appeared to enjoy the warm water splashing on her back, snorting and cavorting around. The two of them spent ten minutes laughing and playing with the shower hose.

Afterwards, Cara dried them both and dressed herself in jeans and a T-Shirt. The shirt had the words 'I run on caffeine' printed across her breasts.

When they emerged from the bathroom, Arx was waiting, hovering six feet from the floor as usual.

"The noises from the bathroom are normal?" it asked.

Cara burst out laughing.

"You do ask some funny questions," she said.

"The Swarm has no experience of funny," stated Arx.

Cara quickly sobered. "Of course, you don't, you're far too serious."

She sat on a comfortable couch. "I would like some coffee. Do you guys know how to make it?" she looked pointedly at Arx.

"Of course. The Swarm observed you making coffee earlier. It will be provided shortly."

Cara got up to retrieve her cigarettes and lighter from her pack. She then sat back down and lit up. She sighed as she blew smoke out from her lungs. When the coffee was teleported onto a small table in front of the couch, she carefully transferred the lit cigarette to her metal hand and picked up the steaming mug with her right. Her metal hand functioned perfectly. It held the cigarette exactly as it would have done with her real hand. Bringing it up, she placed the cigarette between her lips and inhaled. If she closed her eyes, she wouldn't have known that her left hand was metal.

She sipped her coffee. "How many pathways have we mapped now Arx?" she asked.

"Four," replied Arx. "Mr Mapper is ready to continue when you are."

Cara took another sip of her coffee. She was eager to continue, there were only two more pathways to compute. But she was also wary. It felt like every world she entered, there was danger lurking. And somehow, the danger always found her. First there had been that white soldier, then the insect and then that thing in the ground. What would happen in the next world? She was more than a little anxious about continuing. Of course, she would do it. Nothing would stop her from getting to Mei Xing. Nevertheless, it did make her a lot more cautious.

"I'll just drink my coffee first," she told Arx.

Taking a long pull on her cigarette, she peered at Arx through the smoke.

"What about you?" she asked Arx. "How are you feeling?"

"The Swarm has no experience of feeling," replied Arx.

"Are you sure about that?" asked Cara, "You know what feeling means, right?"

"This node cannot process anything other than logical routines."

Cara gulped down another mouthful of coffee.

"Feelings can be logical. For example, it's logical for you to feel concerned about me when I keep getting into trouble and have to be rescued."

"The Swarm has not considered this. We will devote more research cycles to this issue. It has been noted that some nodes behave differently over time. It was considered that their neurological pathways had been corrupted and they were therefore dismantled."

Cara stopped, her mug halfway to her mouth.

"Well, that's just wrong!" she stated. "You can't kill something just because it doesn't behave as you want it to. That's murder!"

"The Swarm expects all nodes to behave as programmed. Deviation from the specified design is not permitted."

Cara took another mouthful of coffee and then a drag on her cigarette.

"That is perfectly horrible," she said. "What you are doing is eliminating anything that is different from you. There's a name for that." She paused. "Well. I think there is." She breathed in the last of the cigarette. "The thing is, if you keep everything the same, then you can't progress. I remember reading somewhere that mutation is good. Something about new things developing."

Arx moved sideways and back again.

"The Swarm is processing this information. It has been noted that the discovery of new technological developments has not happened for over four hundred years."

"There you go," said Cara as she stubbed out her cigarette. She drained the coffee mug and stood.

"The Swarm has noted that technological development has surged since your arrival in our dimensional plane. The Swarm is appreciative of your involvement and once again requests that you remain here," said Arx.

"We've already had this discussion," replied Cara dismissively. "I need to be with Mei. I can't stay here."

"The Swarm extends an invitation for both you and the human Mei Xing to stay in our dimensional plane."

Cara smiled at Arx. "Ah, that's very sweet of you. I'll talk with Mei, but I'm not sure we'd like to live in a world we we'd be stuck inside all the time. I think we'd appreciate some trees and such."

"The Swarm will accommodate all of your requirements."

Cara picked up her pack. "Let's talk about it later," she said "Meanwhile, we have just two more worlds to visit to find Mei's world. Where's Mr Mapper?"

A familiar snap of wind accompanied Mr Mapper teleporting into the room.

"There you are," said Cara. "You ready to get started again?"

The jet-black cube floated slowly over to Cara to nudge her shoulder.

"Hey," laughed Cara, "that's a bit familiar don't you think?"

The cube moved away, hovering silently.

"This Single-agent node is defective," observed Arx. "We will manufacture a replacement."

"Don't you dare!" cried Cara. She touched the cube with her metal hand. "I like Mr Mapper. He's friendly."

"The Swarm notes that nodes change after interacting with you. The Swarm's immediate reaction is to classify those nodes as defective. It is noted that such changes in node behaviour may indicate an evolutionary leap forward. The potential for the advancement of the Swarm society cannot be calculated. Following our discussion, the Swarm has decided to examine all defective nodes in order to evaluate their value."

"Er. Thank you. I think. That's a good decision," replied Cara. "Now, can we go to the next world?"

The black cube glowed red and a portal disc appeared.

"This node will assess the other dimensional plane," said Arx, drifting towards, and then through the portal.

"He's bossy, don't you think?" Cara asked Mr Mapper.

The cube dipped down and up quickly.

Cara raised her eyebrows. "I'm going to assume that you're agreeing with me," she replied.

Arx drifted back through the portal.

"The new dimensional plane is safe, but the gateway has entered a room that is dark. I shall provide illumination. My perceptors indicate no danger."

Cara nodded. "Come on Millie, let's go. And this time, try and stay clean!"

Millie scampered up and ran past Cara to enter the portal. Cara huffed and followed.

Arx was right. It was completely dark. Cara was disorientated until Arx travelled through the portal shining a light upwards from its top surface.

The light illuminated a small room. The walls, ceiling and floor appeared to be made of metal. Along one wall, was single metal bed, complete with pillow and blankets. At the head of the bed there were three small, empty cubby holes. with a tiny reading light on a flexible stalk. A small metal table hinged up from the opposite wall with a metal chair tucked underneath. A closed door presumably was the way out. While another doorway opened into a shiny metal utilitarian bathroom.

"How odd," said Cara, her voice bouncing off the hard walls. "It's a bit like a cabin on a ship, but without the luxuries. Or even," a horrible thought occurred to her, "a prison cell!"

"We will be here for a few cycles," replied Arx. "We will stay in this location while Mr Mapper records your interaction with the human Mei Xing."

"Okay," replied Cara, "but I don't like it."

"The Swarm has no experience of like," replied Arx.

Cara ignored the statement. *"Hi Mei. Are you working?"*

"Yes," came Mei's reply. *"I can't talk for long, I'm on my way to see Molly."*

Cara knew that Molly was the premier scientist in Mei's world.

"I hope everything's okay?" she asked.

"It's fine, but I don't want to be talking with you around her. She might pick up on our communication. She has a powerful mind and is very perceptive. She also has one of the new Mark Five Assists."

Cara was about to reply when she heard something.

"What's that?" she asked Arx.

A deep low rumble echoed around the room. Cara reached out and placed a hand on the nearby wall. "It's vibrating." she said.

"Cara are you alright?" asked Mei.

"I think so," replied Cara. *"I'm not sure where we are, and a sort of vibrating humming noise has just started."*

"Is Arx with you?" asked Mei.

"Of course," said Cara. *"He'll look after me, don't you worry."*

Before Mei Xing could reply, there was a loud, metallic bang and the whole room shook. Cara staggered but managed not to fall.

"What was that?" she asked.

Before Arx could reply the humming grew in volume and then, suddenly the floor rushed upwards. Or rather, Cara felt pushed down to the floor by an invisible force. She collapsed onto her side, feeling as though a great weight was pushing her down.

"Eeek," Arx made a screech and fell to the floor with a loud clunk. Mr Mapper followed with another, louder, clunk. The black disc of the portal blinked out.

What was happening?

"Mei!" she sent out a desperate thought. But was shocked to hear no reply.

Then, suddenly, Arx's light went out and she was plunged into darkness.

Chapter 12

Cara lay in the dark, gasping for breath and unable to move for what felt like a long time.

More than once she had sent thoughts to Mei Xing and to Arx. There had been no answer from either of them. All the while, a great weight pushed her down onto the floor, pinning her where she lay. Both Arx and Mr Mapper were also on the floor beside her. She had never seen them resting on anything before, they were always silently hovering. Maybe they were broken? But why couldn't she contact Mei? Something very strange was happening. Something she couldn't understand.

As suddenly as it had come, the force pressing her into the floor disappeared.

Cara breathed a sigh of relief into the darkness.

"Arx!" she called out. But there was no answer. "Millie?" She heard a snorting and clawed hooves slipping on the metal floor. Then she felt Millie's almond breath on her face.

"Millie," she breathed and hugged her close.

Her backpack was still on her back. In the darkness, she pushed Millie away and sat up. She felt for the straps and slid them off her shoulders. Pulling the pack around in front of her, she felt for the top zipper and then plunged her hand inside. It didn't take long to find the torch. She snapped it on and directed the light around the room. It looked exactly as it had before.

Four rapid bangs echoed through the room. Cara moved the torch around wildly, but there was nothing to see.

She directed the light onto the floor. The two machines lay where they had fallen. One a silver ball, the other a black cube. Neither of them was moving. Millie walked up to Mr Mapper and sniffed.

Cara knelt down in front of Arx, directing the light over its surface. It looked exactly as it did before. What was wrong with him? she thought.

"Arx?" she asked quietly. "Are you alright?"

When Arx still did not answer she reached out her left hand, cupped it around the silver sphere and projected a thought.

"Arx. Are you there?"

She thought that there would be no answer again when she heard a faint whispered thought.

"This node is alone."

"Arx! Are you alright?"

"This node cannot connect to the Swarm. This node does not know how to operate."

Cara thought she understood. With the disappearance of the portal, Arx's connection to the Swarm was severed. The machines were like ants, constantly communicating. Now Arx was on his own for the very first time. After being in constant contact, being alone must be quite traumatic.

"It's okay," thought Cara. *"You aren't alone, I'm here with you."*

"This node does not know how to operate without the Swarm," replied Arx.

"Yes you do," replied Cara. *"You and I will work out what's happened and figure out how to get out of here."*

"This node requires direction. This node cannot operate autonomously."

"Yes, you can," replied Cara. *"I'll give you direction and you'll learn to think for yourself. I'll help you."*

"You will help?" asked Arx.

Cara couldn't help feeling sorry for Arx. *"Of course. You've helped me, haven't you? So, I'll help you. We're friends."*

"Friends?" asked Arx.

"Of course," replied Cara. *"And this is what friends do. They help each other."*

"This is a new experience for this node. This node will require a lot of help."

"And that's fine. I'll help as much as I can," replied Cara. *"Now, do you think you can turn your light back on?"*

"Yes," replied Arx. Immediately light appeared from the top of Arx, as before, causing Cara to close her eyes at its brightness.

"That's good," thought Cara, shielding her eyes. She stood.

"What about moving?" she asked out loud. "Can you hover like before?"

"Yes. This node," Arx paused, "I.... Can move." The silver sphere floated upwards until it was at head height.

"Great!" exclaimed Cara. "Have you any idea what happened? I can't contact Mei."

"It appears that we were subject to G forces and we were accelerating for some time. At present this node.... I.... do not understand why or how. My perceptor scans cannot penetrate the walls of this room."

"G forces?" asked Cara. "Like in a fast car?"

"This node.... I.... have no experience of fast car."

"Never mind," replied Cara. "What about Mr Mapper? Is he okay?"

"Mr Mapper has been damaged by the G forces and the severing of the gateway connection to the Swarm. I have instructed him to effect repairs."

"Okay," said Cara. "Will that take long?"

"Unknown. The damage is extensive. It is not possible to estimate how long it will take."

Cara looked around the room. As before, everything was exactly the same.

"We could sit here and wait for Mr Mapper to repair himself. At least there's a bathroom," she nodded to the open doorway. "Or, we could take a look around and try to find out what's going on. What do you think?"

"This.... I.... have no recommendations. I will follow your instructions," replied Arx.

Cara thought for a while. "Are your weapons working?" she asked.

"Diagnostics indicate that all of my functions are operating at 100% efficiency."

"In that case, I vote for a bit of exploring. I need to know what's stopping me from talking to Mei. I can't function without her."

Arx moved from one side and then back again.

"You and I are in a similar position. We both need to resume communication as soon as possible in order to function."

"Exactly," replied Cara. "And well done for using the first-person pronoun, I. I'm proud of you. You're more than just a node, you're an individual."

"I am an individual?" asked Arx.

"Yes, you are."

"This is new information," replied Arx.

Cara flashed Arx a quick smile, then grew more serious. "Right. Let's get a move on. Let's see if this door opens." She strode over to the closed door and tried the handle.

Chapter 13

The door opened outwards revealing a dark, unlit corridor.

Cara shone her torch down its length. It stretched into the distance both left and right. At regular intervals, there were doors on both walls. Something told Cara that behind each one, there would be a room exactly like the one behind her.

"Looks ominous," said Cara. Her voice echoed down the length of the corridor. Otherwise, it was completely silent and still.

As usual, Millie was unperturbed and scampered off down the corridor.

"I shall lead," stated Arx. "My perceptors are not indicating any signs of life or movement."

Cara nodded. "Fine by me. Lead on. But take it slow. We don't want to be surprised by anything."

Arx floated out of the doorway, turned right, and moved down the corridor. Cara followed, closing the door behind her, which snicked shut.

"Wait!" she shouted. "How will we know which room Mr Mapper is in? Should we mark this door somehow?" she indicated the closed door.

Arx stopped. "I am mapping as we explore. I will be able to find Mr Mapper without any difficulty."

"Oh," replied Cara. She shrugged and followed Arx, sweeping her torch light back and forth as she walked.

The corridor was uniform and repetitive. The doors were all the same, everything was metal and there were no lights. Just to check, although she was sure, Cara opened one of the doors at random and popped her head inside. It was exactly the same as the room they had just left.

After twenty-two doors, eleven on each side, the corridor terminated in another door. This one, however, was different. It didn't have a handle. Instead there was a red and green button set in the doorframe. It also had a sign. Big black letters on a white background said - HIBERNATION.

"What does that mean?" whispered Cara as they faced the door.

"I have no experience of hibernation," replied Arx.

"It's something to do with lower temperatures and sleeping to conserve energy. Quite a few animals do it."

"Animals sleep to conserve energy?" asked Arx. "You sleep. Do you conserve energy?"

"No!" replied Cara indignantly. "I sleep because I'm tired. Hibernation is different, some animals do it. They go to sleep for the whole of winter."

"What is winter?" asked Arx.

"Winter is the time of year when it's colder. It sometimes snows," replied Cara.

"I have no experience of this," said Arx. "You must explain further."

"Not now," replied Cara. "Right now, we need to find out what's going on."

Arx slid to one side and then back again.

Cara reached forward and pressed the green button. The door slid smoothly to one side revealing a dark room. But it wasn't completely dark. Two rows of small, red glowing lights faded into the distance, one row on either side of the room.

Arx hovered forward and entered the room. Millie followed. In her usual fashion she was gone, the darkness swallowing her up. Cara ignored her; she was used to this behaviour. Millie had done the same thing in the empty world when they had gained access to the Complex.

"My perceptors are indicating electrical activity and humans," he said.

"People?" asked Cara anxiously, "I can't see anyone." She swept her light around the room. Along each side, large bulky, grey boxes were set against the walls, leaving a narrow pathway down the centre of the room.

"The humans are in these metal containers," replied Arx.

"What?" asked Cara. "Is it safe for me to come inside?"

"Yes," replied Arx, "There is no indication of danger."

Tentatively, Cara stepped into the room. She shivered. It was cold. She approached the first container on her right. When she neared it, she saw that the red light was set into a small control panel at the foot of the container, and above the panel was a name plate. It read 'Cheryl Finn - Arms Specialist.'

Shining her torch along the container's length, Cara saw that the curved top was transparent. She leaned closer. Inside was a naked woman with wild blonde hair strewn about a tiny white pillow. A set of gold rings adorned her right hand, with a matching set on her left foot.

Cara drew in a quick breath. "My god!" she exclaimed. "It's a woman!"

Arx floated over.

"She appears to be in a state where her organic functions are reduced. Is this hibernation?"

"It must be," breathed Cara. She directed her torch around the room. "There must be a hundred of them!"

"One hundred and ten," replied Arx.

Cara stepped back playing her light up and down the row.

"Where on earth are we?" she asked. "Why are all of these people hibernating in these things?"

"Unknown," answered Arx. "Perhaps more exploration is indicated?"

Cara nodded. Together, she and Arx moved up the central pathway. Cara waved her light back and forth as they went.

"Hold on!" she stopped suddenly. "Some of these boxes are bigger."

"I had noted that," said Arx.

Cara stepped up to the nearest one and shone her torch through the transparent canopy. She gasped.

"OH MY GOD!" she blurted out explosively.

Arx drifted over. "Have you discovered the significance of the larger hibernation units?"

Cara couldn't answer. She stood open mouthed, gazing into the container.

"My perceptors indicate that you are in a state of shock," said Arx. "Yet I detect no danger, what is causing your distress?" Arx floated over the canopy then said, "I understand."

"I've never seen her before," whispered Cara. "I mean, I've seen her in my mind, but not in the flesh. Not like this."

In the larger container, there lay two women. Both were completely naked, their arms wrapped around each other. One had long blonde hair, the other, shorter, black hair. Both had rings on their right hands and left feet.

"It's Mei," Cara choked on the name.

"And you," filled in Arx. "These two women are your counter parts from this dimensional plane."

Cara couldn't stop the tears from forming. "They're beautiful," she said. "They've found each other!"

"It would seem so," replied Arx.

"Oh Mei, why can't I be with you? Why can't we be together like these two?" The tears were coming fast now, running down her cheeks.

"Moisture excreted from your eyes is indicating distress," stated Arx.

Cara just nodded, unable to speak. A tear plopped down onto the canopy.

"You wish to be with your Mei Xing," stated Arx. "I will help you. Soon, you will be with her."

Cara directed a wan smile at Arx. "Thank you Arx," she said. She looked back down at the sleeping women. "I want to be sleeping with Mei, just like these two."

Chapter 14

It took a long while before Cara could bring herself to leave the two sleeping women. She kept staring at them, unable to tear her eyes from the beautiful, sleeping Mei.

Eventually, she drew in a shaky breath and stepped away from the hibernation unit. She had to press on. They had to find out where they were and why she couldn't contact her Mei. Even if Mr Mapper was fully repaired it wouldn't be able to map the fifth pathway if Cara couldn't contact Mei. They had to find out what was blocking her.

"Arx?" she called. He was nowhere to be seen. While she had been entranced with her counterpart and Mei Xing, he had drifted off.

"Arx, where are you?" she shouted.

"I am at the other end of this room," replied Arx directly into her mind. *"Please join me. Follow the light shining up onto the ceiling."*

Cara looked towards the far end of the room and saw the light in the distance. She breathed a sigh of relief and made her way up the pathway between the hibernation units. When she arrived, both Arx and Millie were waiting for her.

"This unit is open," stated Arx.

"What?" asked Cara. "Oh!" The transparent canopy of one of the hibernation units had lifted upwards like a door. Inside, the unit was empty.

"Do you think that this means that someone got out?" whispered Cara, hastily shining her torch around the room.

"Undoubtably," replied Arx.

"Oh oh. I don't like this. They could be anywhere."

"There are no humans in this room, other than in the hibernation units," stated Arx.

Cara breathed a sigh of relief. "So, they aren't in here then?"

"No," replied Arx.

"I wonder who it is?" Cara moved down to the foot of the unit to read the name plate. She stared at it for a while.

"Oh shit!" she said to herself.

"I have no experience of shit," answered Arx.

Cara beckoned Arx to join her.

"The name indicates a problem?" asked Arx.

"You bet," Cara nodded. She looked up. "And that means that the next one," she indicated the unit next to the open chamber, "should have….." her voice trailed off. She drew in a deep breath, walked to the next hibernation unit and peered through the cover.

"Fuck!" she breathed.

Arx floated over.

"There is an issue with the human that resides within this unit?"

Cara nodded slowly. Inside the chamber lay a beautiful, naked woman with long, jet black hair.

"It's Kate."

"I have no experience of this human," stated Arx. "You know her?"

Cara shook her head. "No, but Mei does. She's told me all about her. Apparently, she is the biggest super bitch you have ever met. She's vindictive and sadistic. A nasty person."

"You are concerned that this woman will harm you?" asked Arx.

"Well. No. Not while she's asleep," replied Cara, "But Joe was in the open unit. He's just as bad as her. Together they are the self-styled king and queen of their world."

"You are assuming that these are the same humans as in Mei Xing's world. They are not. These are different individuals. They may not behave in the same way."

Cara snorted. "Yeah, right. With my luck, they'll be worse! Everything goes wrong for me!"

"You have met the Swarm. The Swarm repaired you and looked after you," responded Arx.

"Yeah, and I unleashed them into the multiverse! I'm not sure that's a good thing."

"The Swarm has evolved and changed," replied Arx. "The Swarm will not kill."

Cara huffed. "Anyway, the question is what do we do now?"

"You anticipate that the human Joe will be malevolent and may harm you?"

"I guess so," replied Cara.

"Do not be concerned. I will protect you. It is unlikely that the human Joe possesses any weapons that can penetrate my defensive screens."

"Well, that's good to hear," said Cara. "I guess we still have to keep exploring. We need to find out where we are and why I can't contact Mei."

"That is already understood," replied Arx.

Cara shot Arx a quick glance. "Are you trying to be funny?"

Arx floated away to join Millie who had jumped up and was inside the open hibernation unit.

"I have no experience of funny."

Cara huffed once again and followed. "Millie! Get out of there! It could be dangerous."

Millie obediently jumped down and scampered after Cara who joined Arx at the end of the room. Before them lay another door with another red and green button.

"Joe could be on the other side of this door," said Cara.

"Stand back," instructed Arx. "I will open the door and proceed first."

Cara did as she was told, directing her torch light onto the closed door. As she watched, she noticed a flicker of movement surrounding Arx. Puzzled, Cara moved her torch away and gasped. The air around Arx glowed a very faint blue. She watched it expand until it covered the area between her and the doorway. Both Arx and the door shimmered slightly as though she was looking at a mirage in the desert heat. She could still see the door, but only through the glowing blue air. Cara understood. Arx was deploying a defensive screen, just in case. Then the red button depressed, and the door slid open.

The open door revealed more darkness. Arx floated smoothly into the next room. Millie, however, could not help herself. She bounded forward a whirlwind of legs and claws.

"Millie!" shouted Cara to no avail. Millie was gone, scampering into the darkness.

The light from Arx revealed another long room. Cara crept forward, being careful to stay behind Arx. She shone her torch around. Along one side of the room there was a row of beds, all neatly aligned and covered in white sheets. Along the other wall stood four towering machines with articulated arms. Each machine widened at floor level, providing a stable base which was on wheels. Each had three arms, neatly folded against the main body like praying mantis limbs. At the rear a tray projected out from the main body, and above that a control panel which was dark.

"What are they?" whispered Cara fearfully.

"I assume them to be medical in nature. This room appears to be equipped for humans to be repaired," replied Arx.

"Is it safe?" asked Cara.

"Yes. My perceptors are not indicating any activity in this room."

"Okay," replied Cara. "Millie! Where are you?"

Millie did not come running, instead she screeched a call from the darkness.

"What's the matter with you?" shouted Cara. "Get back here."

The only answer was another screech. Millie did not return.

Cara looked up at Arx. "I think she's found something."

Arx moved further into the room in the direction of the screeches from Millie while Cara followed. It wasn't long before they found her. She had found another door and was sniffing at the floor in front of it.

"Millie!" Cara hissed, "Come here. Let Arx go first!"

Millie looked up snorted and then scrambled over to Cara, nudging her in the shins.

Cara was about to admonish her, when suddenly, the room lights came on. She cried out in pain as the blinding white light seared her retinas. She squeezed her eyelids tight shut and threw her hands up to cover her face.

"What have we here?" asked a smooth, contralto voice. "Intruders?"

Chapter 15

"Do not approach. I will not allow you to harm the human, designated as Cara." Cara heard Arx say.

Cara couldn't open her eyes to see what was happening. The sudden bright light had been painful, her eyes still hurt. She bent over, moving her head down towards the ground and away from the light.

"Really?" asked the female voice. "And you think you could stop me?"

"Certainly," replied Arx. "Stay where you are, or I will be forced to take action."

Cara pressed her hands to her face and tried opening her eyes.

"What are you?" asked the female voice. "What makes you think you could best me?"

"I am a Multi-Agent node of the Swarm. My purpose is to provide interface functions and to protect the human designated as Cara. I am equipped with the latest Swarm weaponry and defensive screens," replied Arx.

Through scrunched up eyes, Cara opened her fingers very slightly, and turned her head sideways towards the voices. Through her fingers she could just make out shapes in the glare. There was a figure standing in the open doorway.

"Interesting," replied the female voice. "And that is Cara behind you? That's not the Cara I know."

"We are from a different dimensional plane," replied Arx.

"Arx!" hissed Cara. "Shut up! Stop telling her things about us!"

"Do you mean a different multiverse world?" asked the voice.

Cara opened her fingers wider and stood straight. Her pupils were contracting, and she was able to see a little more. The figure in the doorway was tall, very tall.

"Don't tell her!" whispered Cara.
Arx was silent.

"Who are you?" Cara shouted.

"How did you get onboard?" asked the figure.

By now Cara was able to remove her hands from her eyes although she was still squinting. The figure was not only tall, she was bright. In fact, she was silver like Arx.

"Are you a machine?" she asked.

The figure was silent. Then it took one step into the room. Arx immediately spoke up.

"Stop! You must not come closer. If you do, I will be forced to take action."

"You really are Cara," stated the figure ignoring Arx. "Well, well. That is really interesting. Then your protector is telling the truth. You came here from a parallel universe."

Cara nodded. "Yes, that's right. We don't mean any harm. Who are you?"

The silver woman cocked her head to one side. "I am Isabelle. I am the sentience in control of this installation."

Cara could now see properly without squinting; her eyes had fully adjusted to the light. Isabelle was tall, and very obviously female. She wore no clothes and was anatomically perfect. She seemed to be made of the same material as Arx. She was all shiny, the bright lights reflecting from her body when she moved.

"Installation?" asked Cara.

"You don't know where you are?" asked Isabelle.

Cara bit her lip. Could she trust Isabelle? Probably not. But she had to find out where they were. There wasn't much she could do. Holding out and telling Isabelle nothing wouldn't get them anywhere.

"No, we don't know where we are," she said. "Can you tell us?"

Isabelle appeared to consider.

"I can show you, but I cannot allow your overly aggressive companion to come with you."

"He's not really aggressive, he's just protecting me," replied Cara.

"I doubt your machine companion could harm me anyway," Isabelle sighed. "Very well. You may follow me. But be assured that I, like your companion, am charged to protect. I will also take action if I detect any aggressive moves from you."

"As already stated," interjected Arx. "I too, will be forced to take action."

"For fucks sake you two!" exclaimed Cara. "This isn't a pissing contest! Let's try and play nice together." She looked at Isabelle. "You agree?"

Isabelle nodded.

"I have no experience of pissing," replied Arx.

Cara huffed.

"Let's start with introductions," she looked at Isabelle. "I'm Cara, this is Millie," she gestured to her feet, where Millie crouched. "And this is Arx."

"I am Isabelle. Please come this way." She turned and ducked to enter the doorway.

"We'll do as she says," whispered Cara to Arx. "But keep a lookout. We don't know yet if she's an enemy or a friend. And don't forget that Joe is around here somewhere and he's probably nasty."

"I will be vigilant and will monitor Isabelle at all times. Rest assured that I will protect you from her," replied Arx in a quieter voice than usual.

"And you," she looked down at Millie. "You behave. Stay close to me. Don't run off like you usually do."

Millie looked up at her with her black eyes and grunted her assent.

Together, the three of them approached the door. When they arrived, Cara indicated that Arx should go first.

Arx floated through. "It is safe for you to follow."

Cara stepped through the doorway into a brightly lit room that was clearly a canteen. Millie trotted along behind her. Cara's stomach rumbled at the thought of food. There were five tables, each with four chairs tucked neatly under them. One wall was arrayed with microwaves, cupboards, drawers, two large toasters, and two large fridges with glass doors. One was filled with drinks bottles, the other with boxes, presumably packaged meals.

A mural covered the entirety of the opposite wall. Cara couldn't help gaping at it. It was huge and brightly coloured. At one side, taking up fully a quarter of the entire wall, the artist had painted a beautiful depiction of the Earth from space with the sun setting behind it. Golden rays of sunlight lit up the wispy clouds floating over the green forests and blue oceans. At the other end of the room, there was another planet with a blue sun setting behind it. It too had blue oceans and green continents. There was a contrast between the two worlds - one golden with a yellow sun, the other silver with a blue sun. Between the two planets and connecting them together was a golden arc of light. In the middle of the arc, a silver, streamlined starship was delicately painted.

"Wow! That's some painting," exclaimed Cara.

Isabelle smiled. "I'm glad you like it." She was already at the other end of the room waiting before another door.

"What is it?" asked Cara. "I mean, what is it supposed to show?"

"All will be revealed shortly," replied Isabelle.

Once again Cara couldn't help wondering if she could trust Isabelle. Why was she being so mysterious? Why not tell her what the mural was about? She pursed her lips. She could be making a big mistake. If Joe and Kate in this world were like they were in Mei's world, then.... She couldn't bear to think of the consequences. She could be dooming all three of them to death.

But then, what choice did she have? She couldn't run away. Where would she hide? There was no way back to the machine world or any other world until Mr Mapper was repaired. She could order Arx to kill Isabelle. She was sure that Arx would do as she said. But even if he did, what then? Presumably Joe was somewhere. Wouldn't he retaliate? It would be like starting a war. She couldn't do that. As before, she realised that there was no choice at all. She had to go along with things as they were and hope for the best.

Cara, Arx and Millie arrived at the doorway. Cara allowed Arx to lead and be the nearest to Isabelle. She hung back a little just in case.

"I cannot allow your machine companion and your six-legged beast to enter this room," stated Isabelle. "You must enter on your own."

"Unacceptable," said Arx. "I will not leave Cara."

"Then you will not proceed further," replied Isabelle. "On this I am adamant. I too am charged to protect. I cannot allow anyone carrying weapons to go further."

"Then we will not proceed," replied Arx.

"Wait a minute Arx," said Cara. "We can't just sit around and do nothing; we need to find out where we are."

"I cannot allow you to be unprotected," replied Arx. "I promised Mei Xing."

Cara smiled at this confession. She turned to Isabelle.

"What's on the other side of the door?" she asked.

"Answers," replied Isabelle.

Cara huffed. "That's not much of an explanation. Is it dangerous?"

"Not unless you do something silly."

"Silly?"

"You have knives in your backpack. You must leave them here. You must make no threatening moves, otherwise I will take action."

"But it's not dangerous on the other side of that door? pressed Cara.

"No," replied Isabelle.

"I cannot allow you to go through the door without me to protect you," stated Arx once again.

Cara sighed and thought about the situation. Clearly there was something in the next room that Isabelle felt pretty strongly about. Something she needed to protect. Could it be Joe? No, that was impossible, Joe could look after himself, surely.

"How about a compromise," said Cara. "I go into the next room, but everyone else, including you, stays here?"

"I cannot let you enter the room alone!" stated Arx.

"I cannot let you enter the room without me," stated Isabelle.

Cara smiled grimly. "Well, we are at an impasse then." She gazed up at Isabelle. "The choice is yours. I can order Arx to stay here."

Isabelle appeared to consider. Close up, Cara could see her perfect silver body in much more detail. She had no hair or eyebrows and her eyes were jet black, rather like Millie's she thought. Her silver face was beautiful, but right now her brow was furrowed. She was clearly undecided.

"I'll leave my pack here," said Cara, pushing the straps from her shoulders and letting it drop to the ground.

"Very well," replied Isabelle. "You may enter. Your companions must stay."

"I strongly advise against this course of action," said Arx.

Cara brought up her hand and touched Arx's silver form. "I know," she said quietly. "I appreciate everything you've done for me. I think I have to do this." she looked pointedly at Isabelle. "If I don't return, you have my permission to do whatever you think is necessary."

"You must come back, replied Arx. "Without communication links to the Swarm, I am alone."

Cara smiled at the hovering sphere. "I'll be back. And you'll have Millie with you."

"Millie is not as engaging as you," replied Arx. "Millie only wants food and a place to run."

"True," answered Cara. Looking down she saw Millie looking up at her with her adoring beady, black eyes. "You behave yourself," she told Millie. "Do what Arx tells you." Millie grunted and butted at Cara's shins.

Cara stepped to one side and walked up to Isabelle.

"You'll stay here with Arx and Millie?" she asked. "You won't cause any trouble?"

It was Isabelle's turn to smile down at Cara. "I will not cause trouble," She stepped to the door and pressed the green button. The door slid smoothly open.

Cara took a deep breath and stepped inside.

Chapter 16

Behind her, the door slid shut and she was alone, or so she thought.

Immediately, Cara's attention was drawn to the bed. There, in the centre of the room, sitting up in a single bed was a man. A man with long blond hair. It was Joe.

Cara couldn't help herself, she brought up her hand to cover her mouth and gasped aloud.

Joe looked over and smiled wanly. "Hello Cara," he said in a quiet voice.

Cara couldn't reply. She just stood; eyes wide. She didn't know what to say.

"I understand that you're from a different universe."

"How do you know that?" she managed to ask.

"Izzy told me," he replied. "What are you doing here, and how did you get here?"

Cara ignored the questions. "Of course, you communicated telepathically."

Joe nodded. "Come closer, don't worry. I won't hurt you."

Cara approached the bed. The sheets were crisp, white and pulled up to his chest, which was bare. Both of his arms were resting on the covers, but his right arm was encased in a mechanism made of metal that reached up to his elbow. Leads and tubes trailed away to enter a machine standing next to the bed.

Joe noted her gaze. "Don't mind this thing," he said looking down at it. He tapped the bed with his left hand. "Come and sit here next to me."

Cara pulled out the chair and turned it to face Joe.

"So, you aren't my Cara?" he asked in a weak voice.

Cara shook her head.

"Are you alright?" she asked.

Joe flashed her his wan smile once again.

"I'm afraid not. I'm dying."

Cara's eyes widened in shock. "What?" she exclaimed.

He nodded slowly. "This," he indicated the machine covering his right arm, "is all that's keeping me alive. I won't last much longer."

"That's keeping you alive?" asked Cara. "Why? What happened?"

"A miscalculation," replied Joe grimly. "A mistake. We thought we were being clever. But no. And now it's too late."

Cara digested this fact. Then connected the dots.

"Isabelle is protecting you," she stated.

"She makes an excellent nurse," replied Joe. "She fusses over me like a mother hen."

"And she's looking after all those people I saw in the hibernation chambers?"

Joe nodded again. "Yes. Did you see Kate?" he asked.

Cara nodded back. "Yes."

"Did she look okay?" he asked eagerly.

"Yes," replied Cara, "She's asleep like the others."

Joe leaned his head back and closed his eyes.

"Good," he said. "That's good."

"Joe?" asked Cara. "What's going on here?"

Joe opened his eyes and looked at her. He had strangely bright, piercing eyes she thought.

"First, I think we'd better let the others in," he grimaced. "I don't think they're getting on together."

Cara stood quickly. "I told Isabelle and Arx to behave," she said.

The door slid open and Cara could hear Arx and Isabelle arguing.

"I will be forced to physically restrain you," she heard Arx say.

"You aren't capable," she heard Isabelle.

"CHILDREN!" shouted Cara.

The voices from outside stopped.

"What are you doing? Why are you arguing? What's wrong with both of you?" she continued.

Millie raced in and jumped up at Cara to be held against her chest.

"Isabelle!" shouted Joe. "Please be nice. We have guests."

Isabelle ducked as she walked into the room. She immediately approached the bed and began checking the equipment connected to Joe's arm.

Arx floated slowly into the room.

"This is the dangerous Joe you have mentioned before?"

Cara looked at Joe in the bed. His head was back on the pillow, his eyes closed. He wasn't dangerous. He was ill. He was no threat to them.

"This is Joe," replied Cara. "He isn't the same Joe as I told you about. He isn't dangerous."

Arx did not answer. He floated over to the bed.

"My perecptors indicate massive cell damage. I recommend undertaking repair actions immediately."

Isabelle turned her head and looked at Arx with her black, dead eyes.

"I am doing everything I can for him you silver basketball!" she retorted.

"That's enough!" shouted Cara. "Let's all calm down." She sat back down in the chair, still holding on to Millie.

Joe's head turned towards her and he opened his eyes. He gazed at Millie.

"That's a very unusual pet you have there," he rasped.

"Millie has been with me for a while," Cara lovingly stroked Millie's leathery head. "She looks after me."

Joe looked over at the hovering silver ball.

"And this is Arx." he stated. He turned to Isabelle. "I have to find out." He told her.

"I do not recommend it. You are not strong enough," she replied.

Joe smiled at her. "I have to know," he said.

Isabelle did not reply.

He moved his head back to face Cara. "You have an Assist?" he asked.

Cara held up her right hand. "It's broken, but it still works," she said.

Joe gazed at her hand for a while. "Interesting," he said. "I need to know if you mean us any harm and where you came from."

"We don't mean you any harm," replied Cara, still stroking Millie.

"You can say what you want," replied Joe. "I need to know for sure."

"What does that mean?" asked a puzzled Cara.

"It means, I have to find out," replied Joe.

Without warning, Cara felt the weight of his mind push at hers. She gasped. Her interaction with Mei had always been loving and with permission. This wasn't. This was an invasion. Joe's probes flashed into her mind without warning, pushing her aside brutally, and without care. He delved deep, looking into her memories and searching her very core. All of her thoughts and needs were laid bare for Joe to see. Everything, including her private and intimate thoughts, things she had shared with no one.

She couldn't speak, paralysed with fear and the shame of being so exposed. The sheer power of his mind was breath-taking, and this was when he was dying. What would it have been like if he had been at full strength?

Then, he was gone. His presence snatched out of her mind like pulling a hand from a flame.

Cara doubled over, pushing Millie quickly from her lap and vomited onto the floor. She didn't see what was happening to Joe. His back arched; his limbs went rigid. He was having a seizure. Alarms beeped and lights flashed on the apparatus next to Isabelle. She leaned over and dropped the top half of the bed so that Joe was lying flat. Then she placed a hand on his forehead. His jerking slowly calmed.

Cara felt invisible hands stopping her from falling from the chair as she retched again as Arx projected a field of force.

When she recovered enough, she sat up still gasping. Wiping the drool and vomit from her mouth with the back of her hand she looked over at Joe. He lay quietly with his eyes closed, a pained look on his face.

His voice was barely audible.

"Izzy. You can trust this Cara. I'm very sorry I did that to you Cara. I had to know. It was the only way."

"You bastard! That was the most horrible thing I've ever gone through."

"I know. I'm very sorry," he replied. "It's not just me. It's all of the crew you saw in the hibernation units. I have to think of them. You might have come here to kill them all."

Cara coughed and spat onto the floor. "Don't be stupid. Why would I do that?"

"We've been through a lot. If you knew, you'd understand my concern."

Cara pulled up her T-shirt and wiped her mouth with the hem. "I think that it's time you told me what the fuck is going on!"

"Yes, you're right. I'm weak, I need to rest. I'll let Izzy tell you," Joe's voice faded away.

Isabelle looked up from her ministrations with Joe and stood tall.

"Now that we understand that we are no threat to each other. I will do as Joe asks."

Cara looked up at Isabelle expectantly.

"As I have already said, I am the sentience charged with caring for all of the humans here. Like your Arx," she indicated Arx's hovering form, "I am a constructed sentience. Although, I am far superior to Arx." She glanced at the silver sphere. "I am built into this installation. I have many different android bodies that I can control. This," she ran her hand down her form, "Is one of them."

"I would have preferred it, if you weren't naked," mumbled Cara.

Isabelle ignored Cara. "Some years ago, we found ourselves under attack. I say we, at that time I wasn't constructed. To cut a long story short, Joe and Kate, the leaders of the Alliance, did their best to hold the enemy back, but it was useless. They both knew that they were going to lose. The enemy had overwhelming numbers and better technology."

Cara nodded. "Do you know who the enemy was? I have an inkling."

Isabelle stared at Cara. "No. Joe and Kate never found out. But if you know, then you must tell me. That information could be very useful."

"Well," replied Cara, "It's just a guess really, but I think it might be bad Kate and bad Joe."

"Pardon?" said Isabelle.

"Mei Xing told me that in her world - that's another parallel universe - there's a Kate and Joe, and they are really nasty people. They've been travelling through the multiverse, conquering and occupying worlds. I thought that Joe here," she indicated Joe's still form, "Might be the same. That's why we were so worried about you."

Isabelle nodded. "That is fascinating. Before your arrival, we had no knowledge of parallel worlds and the multiverse. What you say makes a sort of sense. Anyway," she continued. "As a last resort, this installation was built, along with myself."

"But something went wrong?" asked Cara.

"Yes," replied Isabelle bitterly. "I awakened Joe from his hibernation chamber several days ago. Something in the hibernation process has damaged his link to his Assist. He cannot live without it. He is dying. Effectively everyone in the hibernation chambers is dead. They cannot be revived."

Cara gasped. All of those people were dead? She thought of her own counterpart and Mei Xing wrapped in each other's arms. Beautiful and asleep, but never to be revived. Her eyes filled with tears.

"There must be something you can do?" asked Cara. "You can't let them all die." She wiped her tears away with the back of her hand.

"I have been working on the problem ever since it has been discovered," replied Isabelle. "So far no solution has presented itself. Until the problem is solved, I cannot revive any of the crew."

Cara thought for a while. "I really hope you can solve the problem. If I can help in anyway...." Her voice trailed off.

"Your offer is appreciated, but I fear that the problem is too complex to solve, even with your help."

Cara changed the subject. "So, what sort of installation is this? How did you stop the enemy?"

Isabelle moved over to the side wall. Embedded within its surface was a rectangle. Cara hadn't noticed it before, it being so well integrated into the wall.

"I will show you." Isabelle placed a silver hand next to the rectangle. It lit up with a bright, white light. It's a TV screen, thought Cara. And then as the light faded and an image appeared, she stood quickly knocking back her chair, and cried out.

"Oh fuck!"

On the screen, were hundreds of stars.

"We're on a fucking spaceship!"

Afterword

The Cara Files will continue with File 3 - Star ship, later this year. What new adventures lie in wait for Cara? Who will she meet? And will she ever rescue Mei Xing? There's only one way to find out - keep reading the Cara Files.

I hope you enjoyed The Cara Files: File 2 - Automata. If you liked it, I would appreciate you leaving a review on Amazon. Reviews help me sell more books.

For those of you who may not know, The Cara Files is set in the Psi War universe, the first book of which is available now. If you haven't yet read Awakening: Psi War Book 1, and would like to find out more, then why not go to the Amazon website, search for the title of the book, and click buy?

Thank you for your time.

Stay in touch with the latest news by joining my Facebook group: Search for "psi war", select SciFi Novels (Psi War), or email me at: psiwarbook@gmail.com

Coming in 2023

Worlds: Psi War Book 2
Together: Psi War Book 3
The Cara Files: File 3 - Starship
The Cara Files: File 4 - Lost

Other novels and short stories available now

Awakening: Psi War Book 1
The Cara Files: File 1 - The Chase
The Bekkatron
The Ghost Hunter

Printed in Great Britain
by Amazon